'You do realise that Niko is the heir not just to Petra Innovation but Demetriou Tech?' Alekos met her gaze, his eyes like burning embers, singeing her.

Shocked realisation sliced through her. 'You would recognise him as your heir…?'

'I don't have another.'

'But you might marry,' Iolanthe protested. 'You might have other children—'

'I *will* marry,' Alekos affirmed. 'And I *will* have other children. But Niko is my firstborn son and he will be my heir.'

The coolly stated fact that he would marry put both Iolanthe's head and heart in a spin—which was ridiculous, of course. Alekos was thirty-six years old. Of *course* he would marry at some point—and probably soon. Maybe he even had a woman already, waiting in the wings, ready and eager to become Kyria Demetriou. It had nothing to do with her.

'You sound very sure,' she said after a moment. 'You haven't even met Niko.'

'I know he's my son.'

Iolanthe tried to gather her scattered thoughts. 'But what about this potential bride of yours? She might want the children you have together to—'

'My potential bride—' Alekos cut across her, his voice like a blade '—will want *Niko* as my heir.'

Iolanthe stared at him, flummoxed. 'How—?'

'Because,' he continued implacably, 'my prospective bride—my only bride—is *you*.'

Secret Heirs of Billionaires

There are some things money can't buy…

Living life at lightning pace, these magnates are no strangers to stakes at their highest. It seems they've got it all… That is until they find out that there's an unplanned item to add to their list of accomplishments!

Achieved:

1. Successful business empire

2. Beautiful women in their bed

3. *An heir to bear their name…?*

Though every billionaire needs to leave his legacy in safe hands, discovering a secret heir shakes up his carefully orchestrated plan in more ways than one!

Uncover their secrets in:

Unwrapping the Castelli Secret by Caitlin Crews

Brunetti's Secret Son by Maya Blake

The Secret to Marrying Marchesi by Amanda Cinelli

Look out for more stories in the
Secret Heirs of Billionaires series coming soon!

DEMETRIOU DEMANDS HIS CHILD

BY
KATE HEWITT

First Published in Great Britain 2016
By Mills & Boon, an imprint of HarperCollins*Publishers*
1 London Bridge Street, London, SE1 9GF

© 2016 Kate Hewitt

ISBN: 978-0-263-06521-3

After spending three years as a die-hard New Yorker, **Kate Hewitt** now lives in a small village in the English Lake District with her husband, their five children and a golden retriever. In addition to writing intensely emotional stories she loves reading, baking and playing chess with her son—she has yet to win against him, but she continues to try. Learn more about Kate at kate-hewitt.com.

Visit the Author Profile page
at millsandboon.co.uk for more titles.

CHAPTER ONE

TONIGHT WAS FOR MAGIC. Iolanthe Petrakis gazed at her reflection in the cheval mirror of her childhood bedroom, her mouth curving into a smile of delighted expectation. Her new gown of silvery-white satin rippled over her body, flaring out from her hips and ending in frothy ruffles around her ankles. It was a fairy-tale dress, sparkling whenever she moved, fit for a princess. And tonight she felt like a princess, Cinderella poised for her first ball. She was determined to enjoy every moment.

A light knock sounded on the door. 'Iolanthe?' her father, Talos Petrakis, called. 'Are you ready?'

'Yes.' Iolanthe smoothed her hand over her shining dark hair, drawn up into an elegant chignon by the housekeeper, Amara. Her heart thudded with both excitement and nerves. Taking a deep breath, she turned from the mirror and opened the door to her father.

Talos surveyed her silently for a moment, and Iolanthe held her breath, hoping he was pleased with her appearance. After subjecting her to a lifetime of seclusion at his countryside villa, he was finally allowing her an evening's entertainment and pleasure. She couldn't bear for it to be taken away.

'Is it all right?' she asked when the silence stretched on. She smoothed her hands down the shiny fabric. 'Amara helped pick it...'

'It is suitable.' Talos gave one terse nod of acceptance, which filled Iolanthe with relief. Her father had never been one for physical affection or effusive praise; she'd got used to it. A nod was enough. 'You must conduct yourself with propriety at all times,' he added, his face set into stern lines.

'Of course, Papa.' When had she ever done otherwise? But then, she'd never had a chance to do anything but. Tonight, perhaps… She smothered a mischievous smile, not wanting her father to guess her thoughts. In any case, she'd hardly get up to much. But a little adventure, a little excitement…she craved that, after so many years of solitude.

'Your mother would smile to see you now,' Talos said gruffly, and Iolanthe's heart gave a painful little twist. Althea Petrakis had died from cancer when Iolanthe had been only four years old. The few memories she had of her mother were hazy, no more than a whiff of perfume, the touch of a soft hand. Since her death, Talos had withdrawn from family life and immersed himself in his business. If Althea had lived, Iolanthe had often wondered sadly, would her father have been different, more present, more affectionate? As it was, she only saw him every few months or so, and the visits were short, no more than inspections to make sure she was toeing the line.

'As beautiful as you look,' Talos continued, 'you need something more.' He withdrew a small velvet box from the pocket of his tuxedo jacket. 'This is for a woman full grown, ready for a husband.'

'A husband…' Iolanthe didn't want to think about that. She knew she would have to marry a man of her father's choosing at some point, but tonight she wanted to think of adventure. And yes, maybe a little of romance, but not marriage. Not duty.

'Open it,' Talos commanded, and all worries flew from her head as she flipped the lid of the box and gazed in admiration at the diamond teardrop earrings nestled within. 'They're beautiful.' She'd never had any jewellery of her own; she'd never needed any, living a secluded life in her father's villa in the country.

'There's more.' From another pocket Talos withdrew a matching necklace with three exquisite teardrop-shaped diamonds. 'This was your mother's. She wore it on our wedding day.'

Iolanthe took the necklace reverently, her fingers smoothing over the polished stones as she imagined her mother once touching them in a similar way. 'Thank you, Papa,' she whispered, tears choking her voice. He'd never given her anything like this before, never shown her so much affection.

'I was just waiting for the right moment to give them to you.' Talos cleared his throat, uncomfortable with her obvious emotion. 'It is not every day a young woman attends her first ball. She must be outfitted properly.'

Iolanthe put the earrings in and then turned so her back was to her father. 'Will you fasten the necklace?'

'Of course.' Her father did the clasp and then rested his hands lightly on his daughter's shoulders. 'Lukas will accompany you tonight, and keep you safe. Make sure you show him the proper attention.'

Iolanthe had met Lukas, her father's Head of Tech, a few times, and the thought of spending the entire evening with such a stuffed shirt made her insides wither in disappointment. 'I thought you would accompany me.'

'I have business to attend to. Balls such as these are times to network, not just socialise.' He stepped back, his expression stern once more. 'Lukas is an appropriate companion for you. I am allowing you to attend your first ball because you are old enough, and it is time you had a husband. Lukas would be a suitable choice.'

Lukas? She couldn't imagine anything worse. Yet Iolanthe recognised the hard line of her father's mouth, the flat black of his eyes. She could not argue with him now. Wordlessly she nodded even as a spark of rebellion lit her soul. This was her first ball, perhaps even her only ball, and she had no intention of spending the entire evening, much less the rest of her life, with dull-as-ditchwater Lukas Callos.

* * *

Alekos Demetriou stepped into the ballroom, light from the many crystal chandeliers glancing off diamond-spangled women and black-jacketed men. The best of Athens' society had gathered tonight for the city's first social event of the season, and this time Alekos had been included. A year ago his name would not have been on the exclusive guest list; no one had even known it. But now, after years of setbacks he could hardly bear to think about, he was finally starting to make his way and establish both his business and his name. He had every right to be here, rubbing elbows with the rich and entitled, and he intended to enjoy the privilege to the full.

Plucking a glass of champagne from one of the circulating trays, Alekos narrowed his eyes as he looked around the room, searching, as he always was, for the jovial face of his enemy. Talos Petrakis, the man who had taken everything from him, and done it with a smile on his face, presenting to the world the false front of a benevolent businessman, a genial entrepreneur.

Just the thought of Petrakis made Alekos's insides clench as bitterness surged through him, corroding the remaining fragments of his soul. In those first years after Petrakis's betrayal he'd fought against the overwhelming emotion, the fury and despair and *hurt* he'd felt at the older man's devious actions. Then he'd realised that he could channel that emotion, use it for his own good. For the last four years he'd forged those toxic feelings in a furnace of determination, turning them into a steely, unrelenting drive to succeed. And it had worked.

He was finally reaching a point where he could actually consider how to enact revenge on the man who had stolen everything from him. Coming face-to-face with Petrakis after four long years would be the first step. Unfortunately, he couldn't see the man anywhere.

A flash of white, a crystalline sparkle, caught the corner of his eye and Alekos turned and glimpsed a young woman at the far end of the ballroom. Her slender body was encased in a white gown beaded with diamantés, her face hidden behind an ivory demi-mask like those many of the women wore this evening. Tonight was meant to be a costume ball, but few took it beyond a mask made elegant with jewels, feathers, and silk.

The woman moved, and Alekos admired the way the light gleamed off her blue-black hair, touched the round curve of her cheek and the slender hollow of her throat. She looked pure and lovely in comparison to the more jaded women who circulated the room, affecting poses of boredom. In contrast this woman glowed, like a luminescent, newly discovered pearl nestled amidst a thousand tarnished gems. Her eyes were wide as she gazed around the ballroom, drinking everything in as if she were viewing Aladdin's cave of wonders. Alekos couldn't remember ever looking or feeling that way, as if life was full of possibility, of *wonder*. Maybe he had as a small boy, before life had shown him how hard and grim it could be. How indifferent and cruel people could be.

Despite her obvious interest in her surroundings, the young woman was hugging the wall, too shy or perhaps simply content to be a mere spectator of events. Interest sharpened to a finely honed point inside Alekos and he started towards her. He didn't know who she was, but he intended to find out.

'Alekos.' A meaty hand clapped him on the shoulder and Alekos turned, schooling his expression into an easy smile as he greeted Spiro Anastos, a corpulent CEO who had been one of the first to use his content management software system. 'It is good to see you here.'

'Spiro.' Alekos shook the man's hand. 'It's good to be here.'

'You will have fun tonight, eh? My Sofia always says you work too hard.'

'Perhaps I do.' For the last four years he'd done nothing but work, regularly pulling twenty-hour days and going home only to eat and sleep for a few brief hours, all in order to establish his business and his name. And it had worked. He was twenty-six years old and CEO of his own company that was growing fast.

'Tonight is for pleasure,' Spiro stated. 'Drink, eat, dance.' His eyes sparkled as he threw his arms wide. 'Make love!'

Alekos gave a smiling nod as Spiro let out a belly-deep chuckle. Clearly the older man had been indulging in the first of his commands, and Alekos didn't begrudge him it.

'I'll bear your words in mind,' he murmured and with a nod of farewell he shouldered past Spiro, intent on finding the woman who had captivated him from a distance.

Iolanthe stood on the edge of the ballroom, her mask held up to her face. She'd managed to slip from Lukas when he'd been waylaid by some businessmen, and she had no desire for him to find her again. She'd already endured several dances with Lukas; his hands had been damp, his steps mechanical, and his halting conversation had been about computer software. But at least the music had been lovely and Iolanthe had enjoyed the way her skirt had swirled about her as they'd moved across the floor, the music swelling and crashing over them in a symphonic tide.

Maybe she would dance again tonight. Maybe someone else, someone who could actually look her in the eye and make conversation, would ask her.

She pictured it now: a handsome man striding purposefully across the floor, intent firing his eyes, his mouth curving into a smile of sensual promise as he held out his hand...

A flush spread through her body at the thought, and Iolanthe laughed softly, amused and embarrassed by her own girlish fantasy. Most likely she would stand here in the corner for most of the ball, avoiding Lukas and staying in the shadows, awed by the older and more sophisticated women who tossed back their perfectly groomed heads and uttered tinkling laughs. Well, she could still enjoy that. Just looking at all the women in their gorgeous ball gowns was a delight, especially after a lifetime spent in virtual isolation.

'Good evening.'

Iolanthe stiffened as a figure suddenly loomed in front of her, his voice low and authoritative and strangely sensual. It took her stunned brain a moment to realise he was actually addressing her, and then another few seconds to respond.

'Good...good evening!' She'd instinctively pressed her mask closer to her face, its wire frame nearly cutting into her skin, and now she blinked and peered through the feathered eyeholes to get a better look at the man who had approached her. He was as tall and dark as anything out of her naïve fantasies, she realised with a rush of both excitement and alarm. Well over six feet, the stark lines of his tuxedo jacket emphasising his broad shoulders and impressive chest. Eyes the colour of topaz surveyed her with thorough consideration, while perfectly defined lips that could have graced a Grecian statue curved in blatant male appreciation.

Iolanthe felt as if she'd tumbled down a rabbit hole, into some bizarre and amazing alternate reality. She'd been imagining such a scenario as this, but she'd never thought it would actually *happen*, and certainly not with a man who looked like this one. Iolanthe couldn't decide if he looked more like the hero or villain of one of the romance novels her housekeeper Amara sometimes slipped her. Maybe both.

'I noticed you from across the room,' the man said,

thrilling her all the more. 'And I decided that I had to come and meet you.'

'Really?' Iolanthe cringed inwardly at the surprise audible in her voice, but the man merely smiled, a dimple appearing in his cheek, making him seem slightly less fearsome.

'Really,' he assured her. 'You looked like you were enjoying yourself here in the corner, watching everyone.'

'I've never been to a ball before,' Iolanthe admitted, and then cringed again at how young and gauche she must sound. This man, with his darkly compelling good looks, was going to regret so much as crossing a room to meet her. The truth was she had no idea what to say to him, no experience of men or flirting or life at all. And she was awestruck. Who wouldn't be, though, with a man as powerfully charismatic and attractive as this one? She was tempted to touch him to see if he was real.

'Perhaps you would tell me your name?'

'Oh, yes, of course.' Flushing, Iolanthe stumbled on. 'It's Iolanthe. And you are…?'

'Alekos. Alekos Demetriou.' His smile curved deeper, his gaze flicking over her in what even she in her inexperience knew was masculine assessment. She wondered whether he liked what he saw and realised that she hoped he did. 'Would you care to dance?'

'Oh…' Shock made her simply stare for a few delighted seconds. He'd actually asked her to dance, and tonight *was* for magic. She'd wished for magic in her bedroom, had dared to dream about it, and now it was actually real. The whole world seemed to sparkle, promise shimmering in a haze of possibility. Here was her adventure, her excitement. Her romance.

'I…' For a second Iolanthe considered her father, his stern instructions for her to behave properly and stay with Lukas. But what was the harm in a dance? That was why she'd come to the ball, was it not? She had the rest of her life to be the dutiful daughter, the obedient wife.

Tonight she wanted to *live*. The spark of rebellion that had lit her soul hours ago now burst into flame.

'Well?' Amusement laced Alekos's voice and he arched one eyebrow, his hand still outstretched, long, tapered fingers reaching towards her.

'Yes,' she said firmly. 'Yes, I would love to dance.'

Alekos's insides jolted as Iolanthe's palm slid across his, his whole body suffused with a sudden, surprising desire.

He'd started to regret engaging the young ingénue in conversation from almost the moment they'd met—she was clearly very young and even more innocent. And also beautiful—even with the demi-mask pressed to her face, Alekos could appreciate her delicate bone structure and flawless skin, the curves of her cheek and neck graceful and pure. From behind the diamanté-encrusted mask, eyes the colour of moonlight on water regarded him with heartbreaking honesty. Iolanthe, it seemed, had not yet learned to dissemble. And although she was young her body possessed womanly curves, and the sparkling white satin dress hugged each one lovingly.

Her silver-grey eyes widened as Alekos drew her towards him, and he knew she too felt that jolt of desire that had unsettled him. His work had not allowed him time for a social life, and so he'd had his sexual needs met in the most expedient way possible—with a series of one-night stands or brief affairs with experienced women, most of them as jaded as himself, none of whom were looking for more than simple physical need quickly sated. Iolanthe definitely did not fit into that category.

One dance, Alekos told himself. One short dance and then he would smile and walk away from a woman he had no business being interested in.

The band struck up a tune as Alekos guided Iolanthe to

the dance floor. She came gracefully, her head held high, her eyes shining like silver stars. And when Alekos turned and brought her body in close and exquisite contact with his, she moulded herself naturally to him, her hips and breasts nudging him as they both swayed.

Sweat prickled on his forehead. Desire roared through his veins, a surging tidal wave of need that shocked him with its intensity. He'd never reacted to a woman so instantly and overwhelmingly and all he could think was, *Why her? Why now?*

She was beautiful, yes, and charming, if a little youthful and shy. There was an innate loveliness to her face, and he liked the openness he saw in her eyes as she glanced around the room, a small, wistful smile curving her lush pink mouth. But to feel this way...to imagine plucking the pins from her hair and letting the dark locks tumble down her shoulders, to envision plundering that pink mouth with his own, fitting her hips snugly against his...

Silently Alekos swore. The last thing he needed to do was fan that dangerous flame by picturing such things. He tried for a polite smile instead.

'So, Iolanthe, are you from Athens?'

'My father has a house here, but I've lived most of my life in the country.' She tilted her head up to smile at him, her nose wrinkling and a new, wry expression lighting her eyes. She still held the mask to her face like the security blanket it so obviously was; her other hand rested lightly on his shoulder, a butterfly's touch. Alekos had already fitted his palm to the delicate dip of her waist, his fingers fanning out along her hip. He could feel the warmth of her through the thin satin of her dress, felt her tremble slightly in his loose embrace.

'The country?' he prompted, determined to keep the polite chit-chat going and in doing so cool down his libido.

'My father's estate,' she clarified with another appealing wrinkle of her nose.

'Ah.' A rich young heiress, no doubt, kept behind high walls until she was brought out to be admired and duly married off.

Iolanthe laughed, the sound surprisingly low and throaty, and filled with genuine humour. 'Yes, it is as boring as it sounds. I've been packed off to the country, practically wrapped in cotton wool. And now I suppose you will think me a dull conversationalist indeed.'

'Not at all,' Alekos returned smoothly. 'I find you refreshing.'

'Which makes me sound like a drink of water.'

'Or the finest champagne.' His gaze met hers and he saw awareness and heat flicker through her eyes. Why was he flirting with her? He didn't seem to be able to resist. 'Will you return to the country after this ball?'

'Almost certainly, but I'd like to stay in Athens.' Her face softened, her gaze distant. 'I'd like to *do* something.' A tiny sigh escaped her. 'I feel like I've spent my whole life waiting. Have you ever felt like that?' She lifted her gaze to his, and Alekos started at the wistful openness he saw there, the vulnerability and honesty he saw that he always fought so hard to hide in himself.

'Sometimes,' he allowed. The last four years had been a slow burn of waiting. Revenge was a long game. But he had no intention of telling Iolanthe any of that. 'What are you waiting for?' he asked. Marriage, no doubt, to someone dully appropriate.

'For excitement,' Iolanthe answered immediately, and Alekos heard both longing and eagerness in her voice. 'Adventure—it doesn't have to be something big. I'm not looking to scale mountains, or—I don't know—pan for gold.' She laughed, and again that throaty sound had desire sweeping through him, heat pooling in his groin. 'Now I really sound like a fool.'

'You don't,' Alekos assured her. She sounded young and hopeful and completely sincere. It was a surprisingly heady combination. 'But what kind of adventure do you mean?'

'Something...something that makes life worthwhile. Important, even.' Iolanthe's voice turned determined as her hand clenched instinctively on his shoulder. Alekos felt a corresponding surge of protectiveness that he barely understood. Yes, she was young and impressionable and naïve, but she was also a stranger. Why did he care? Why did it alarm him to think of her fragile dreams being shattered by the harsh realities of life? Just as his had once been, a cruel blow had left him reeling for years.

'Important?' he prompted, an edge entering his voice. Dancing with this wisp of a girl, hearing her whisper her dreams, was presenting him with far more of both an emotional and physical challenge than he'd ever anticipated. He wanted her in ways he couldn't even begin to contemplate. He wanted to make her laugh again, and he wanted to kiss that soft pink mouth.

'I suppose everyone wants to feel important,' Iolanthe answered with a dismissive shrug of her slim shoulders. 'And it's not that I want to be important myself...I couldn't care less about that. But I want to do something that makes a difference to somebody, even if it's just something small. I want to live, not just watch other people do it, my nose pressed up against the glass.' She laughed, and this time the sound was tinged with bitter resignation. 'But what does it matter? I'm only likely to end up married.'

The simply stated truth, one he'd already arrived at himself, now had him tensing in instinctive resistance. 'Why do you say that?'

She tilted her head to look up at him, the sparkle leaving her eyes, her mouth flattening. 'I'm twenty years old and my father intends to choose my husband. The only reason I'm at this ball is to show myself off to suitable men.' She practically spat the words out, her hand clenching on his shoulder.

'Does he have one in mind?' Alekos asked, hating the thought.

'Maybe.' Her expression tightened and she glanced away. 'But I want to have some say in the matter.'

'As you should.'

'I don't know if my father agrees.' She sighed, the sound too weary for a young woman whose life should stretch ahead of her with nothing but promise and possibility. 'But let's not talk about that. I can't bear to think about it, not when tonight is the only time I might be able to have fun and enjoy myself with the most handsome man at the ball.' Her smile turned deliberately coquettish, and he saw the humour in her eyes, the acknowledgement that she was flirting shamelessly. It made him smile.

'Indeed,' he murmured, and whirled her about the dance floor.

'I must sound ridiculous,' Iolanthe said with another little laugh, her head tilted back so she could look up at him. 'Wittering on about being important and changing things.'

'You don't sound ridiculous.' Hadn't he once been the same, burning with ambition, flying high on hope? Then he'd come crashing to the ground, and now the only thing he burned for was revenge. 'I think everyone wishes to make a difference in life,' he told her.

'And you?' She glanced up at him, her expression all open curiosity. 'How would you like to make a difference?'

Alekos hesitated, wondering how much to reveal. 'I want to see justice done,' he said finally, for that was certainly true. He wanted Talos Petrakis to pay for his crimes.

Iolanthe gave him a small smile. 'That certainly seems a worthy goal. Far more than I'll ever achieve, I'm sure.'

'Who knows what you might do?' Alekos returned. 'You are young, with your whole life in front of you. You don't have to marry if you don't want to.'

She pursed her lips, considering his statement with perhaps too much seriousness. Who was he to encourage this naïve socialite to rebel? 'What would I do if I didn't marry?'

'You could get a job. Go to university, even. What subjects did you like at school?'

'I was tutored at home, but I always enjoyed art.' She laughed. 'Not that I possess enough talent to become a proper artist.'

'You never know.'

'You seem very optimistic.'

He laughed, the sound harsh. That was one adjective that would never be attributed to him. 'I just don't like to see a young woman such as yourself closing down all her possibilities.'

She smiled wryly. 'I'm sure I seem very young and naïve compared to most of the women here.' She nodded towards the crowd of sophisticated guests.

'Most of the women here are jaded,' Alekos said. 'You are a breath of fresh air.' Although he'd intended the words as mere flattery, he realised they held truth. Iolanthe's inability to dissemble, the very innocence that had put him off, now intrigued and intoxicated him. He was disillusioned himself; he no longer trusted or cared for anyone. What would it be like to feel as Iolanthe yearned to, as if the world held nothing but possibility and hope? Once he'd felt it, as a child, but it seemed so long ago now he could barely remember the emotion, the happiness. He realised he didn't want Iolanthe to lose her optimism, no matter what the future held for her. He didn't want the flame he saw burning inside her to be extinguished so quickly on the altar of familial duty.

The music ended and yet Alekos was loath to walk away from Iolanthe as he'd intended to do earlier. And so, against all better judgment, he found himself asking instead, 'Would you care to get some air on the terrace?'

'A real breath of fresh air?' Iolanthe teased, her eyes

sparkling. Alekos conceded her point with a rueful nod, holding his breath as he waited for her acquiescence.

Iolanthe's gaze skirted the ballroom before returning to rest on him. She squared her slender shoulders as if making a decision. 'Yes,' she said. 'I would like that very much.'

Magic. Everything about this encounter with Alekos Demetriou felt magical, surreal, as if Iolanthe would wake up at any moment and find herself back in her bedroom, the evening yet to begin.

She'd enjoyed their conversation, had found her insecurities falling away as Alekos had looked at her with such blatant male admiration, but, more importantly, had listened to what she'd said—and had seemed to understand. His words thrilled her, because they made her wonder and even hope that there might be more to her life than what her father demanded and everyone expected—marriage to a man of his choosing, most likely Lukas Callos.

But she wouldn't think of that now. Alekos took her hand as he led her towards a set of French windows that had been left open to the evening air, and the slide of his palm across hers made her insides quake like jelly. Was it normal to react to a handsome man like this? She certainly hadn't reacted to Lukas this way. And she barely knew Alekos. In truth she didn't know him at all. Yet his smile made her sway, and the touch of his hand set her heart to hammering, giving her a new, buoyant sense of hope. How was it possible?

Alekos pulled aside the window's gauzy curtain as Iolanthe stepped through onto the terrace. She rested one hand on the stone balustrade, breathing in the warm, dusty air as the sounds of the night settled around her—a distant beeping of a car's horn, the strains of music from the ballroom. A woman's laughter, low and throaty, and a man's answering murmur.

The nape of her neck prickled as Alekos joined her, his shoulder nudging hers as they both looked out at the night. The Acropolis, lit up against a dark sky, was a stunning backdrop to the narrow streets and terraced buildings of the Plaka.

'So I don't actually know anything about you,' Iolanthe said with a little laugh. 'Besides your desire for justice.'

Alekos slid her a sideways glance. 'What would you like to know?'

Everything. Anything. They'd shared only one dance, and yet this man captivated and enchanted her. 'You live in Athens?'

'Yes.'

'What do you do? For work, I mean?'

'I run my own business, Demetriou Tech.'

'Oh. That sounds...' Iolanthe cast for an appropriate word and came up only with '...interesting.'

'It is.'

She thought she heard amusement in his voice, and realised he was probably laughing at her. And she couldn't even blame him. 'I don't know much about IT.' Even though her father's company was IT-based. Talos didn't believe women had any place in the business world; he'd always told her he wanted to shelter her from such concerns.

'I wonder what you will do with your life,' Alekos murmured, 'now that you're waiting for it to begin?'

For a few dazzling seconds Iolanthe imagined other possibilities than marriage: university, work, even travel. 'I'd like to see more of the world,' she said recklessly. 'Go to Paris, maybe, or New York.' She pictured herself along the Seine or in Greenwich Village, working on charcoal sketches and soaking up the atmosphere. She might as well imagine being on Mars. 'I want to see and do things...experience life for myself rather than just watch from afar.'

'Are you experiencing life now?' Alekos asked softly.

His fingers brushed her cheek, making her shiver at the unexpected caress, its startling yet brief intimacy. She felt as if he'd torched her insides, everything going up in a whoosh.

'Yes…' she whispered. She wanted him to touch her again, craved it with a sudden and overwhelming intensity. 'I think,' she said with a nervous little laugh, 'this is the most exciting thing that's ever happened to me.'

Alekos surveyed her with eyes like burning gold; Iolanthe trembled when she saw his gaze drop to her mouth. 'Then perhaps you need a bit more excitement,' he murmured, and then he kissed her.

CHAPTER TWO

HE WAS INSANE. Clearly crazy to kiss this utter innocent, and yet from the moment Alekos's lips touched Iolanthe's he knew he was lost. The sweetness of her response was his undoing; she tensed briefly under his kiss, clearly shocked, one hand fluttering up to clutch at his lapel, and then her mouth opened under his like a flower and he drank of its sweet nectar.

Distantly he heard her gasp in surprise as his tongue swept into her mouth, claiming its softness. Her hand clenched his jacket and the mask dropped from her other hand as her body yielded to his.

Alekos was barely aware of his actions as he backed her up against the balustrade, his hands sliding down the slippery satin of her dress to anchor on her hips and bring her even closer to his arousal.

Another gasp, and far too belatedly he realised what he was doing, practically thrusting his hips against hers. He tore his mouth from hers with a gasp of his own, swearing under his breath as he eased away from her.

'Iolanthe...' She looked up at him, her mouth swollen, her eyes dazed. Without her mask in place she was even lovelier, her skin like ivory blushed with pink, her eyes luminous. Alekos swore again. 'I'm sorry. I didn't mean for that to happen.'

Iolanthe touched her fingers to her lips. 'What *did* you mean to happen?' she asked with a soft laugh, and relief pulsed through him at the realisation that he had not scared or horrified her.

'I wasn't thinking,' he admitted as he stooped to retrieve her mask. 'I intended to walk away from you after our dance, but...' He stopped, reluctant to admit how much this slip of a woman affected him. How much he wanted her.

'I'm glad you didn't,' Iolanthe said. She glanced up at him, her eyes bright, her smile shy. 'That was my first kiss.'

He'd suspected as much, and yet her confirmation made him feel even worse. He'd been halfway to deflowering an innocent virgin, hardly his style at all. This needed to end. Now.

He handed her the scrap of mask; she took it without putting it back to her face. She was looking at him with such open expectation he could hardly bear to meet her gaze. 'I should take you back into the ballroom—'

'Don't, please.' She laid a hand on his chest, and even that gentle touch had Alekos's blood surging again. 'I don't want to go back there.'

'Someone else will ask you to dance—'

'I don't want someone else.' Her eyes darkened. 'Besides, I'll just feel inadequate compared to all those glamorous socialites.'

'You should never feel inadequate,' Alekos answered. 'You were the most beautiful woman in the room.'

'Then stay out here on the terrace with the most beautiful woman,' Iolanthe challenged. Her hand pressed lightly on his chest. 'Please.'

Iolanthe didn't know what had come over her, to make her proposition a man so boldly. Perhaps it was desperation— she couldn't stand the thought of him taking her back to the ball, and having Lukas swoop down once more as her keeper. Or perhaps it was Alekos's kiss that had given her courage—perhaps it had changed her. That moment had felt more like fire than magic, singeing her senses, making her come alive in a way she hadn't even known she could. She wanted him to kiss her again, but she wasn't that bold. Yet.

'Iolanthe…?'

She tensed, her heart seeming to plummet inside her, as she heard Lukas's familiar, nasal voice. *No. Go away, Lukas.*

'Are you…?' Lukas stepped through the windows, stopping when he saw her with Alekos. Iolanthe dropped her hand from Alekos's chest, surprise flaring within her when he stayed it, trapping it with his own, his long, lean fingers wrapping around hers.

'Yes?' he enquired pleasantly, half turning to face Lukas.

Lukas frowned and nodded at Iolanthe. 'Your father wants me to stay with you.'

Of course he did. Her father had made it clear he'd like to see her with Lukas, but surely she had some choice in the matter. Some say in her life.

'Iolanthe…?' Lukas prompted. Iolanthe glanced up at Alekos; he did not look encouraging. His mouth was set in a hard line, a muscle flickering in his jaw. He dropped her hand.

'You should go,' he said flatly and she tried not to let the hurt show on her face. Had he bored of her so easily?

'Iolanthe,' Lukas said again, his voice insistent now, and, even though it was the last thing she wanted to do, Iolanthe stepped away from Alekos. For a second she thought she saw regret flicker in his eyes, and her own resolve wavered. If he said anything to convince her to stay, she would, and damn the consequences.

Then Alekos's expression hardened once more and he looked away as Iolanthe fitted her mask to her face and Lukas led her from the terrace.

'Your father wants us to dance again,' Lukas stated, and Iolanthe glanced at him with weary frustration. She did not want to dance with this man. She certainly didn't want to marry him. But perhaps if she endured a few dances, she'd find a way to escape again. To find Alekos and experience that magic that had made her feel as if life held far more possibility than she'd dared dream.

'All right,' she said, trying not to cringe away from Lukas's slightly damp hand. Alekos's hand had been warm and dry and strong, and he'd moved her around the dance floor with almost arrogant assurance. Lukas's careful, mechanical steps made Iolanthe want to stamp on his foot, or, better yet, flounce away from the dance floor.

She did neither, enduring not one but three dances with Lukas while he shuffled about stoically, barely engaging her in conversation as her gaze moved around the crowded ballroom, searching for that familiar, dominant figure. She didn't see him, and the hope and excitement that had made her insides fizz began to trickle away.

Several hours later Iolanthe's feet were aching along with her heart. She'd danced and then stood with Lukas while he talked business with various guests, always keeping an eye on her, clearly having no intention of allowing her to slip away from him again. She hadn't caught so much as a glimpse of Alekos. Clearly he'd had enough of her. Innocence was probably interesting only for so long.

Now the ball was ending, guests streaming out of the hotel towards the queue of waiting limos and luxury sedans.

'Where is my father?' Iolanthe asked Lukas.

'He's coming shortly. He wants us to wait.'

Iolanthe sighed, wanting only to go home to bed. The excitement of attending her first ball had gone completely flat now that she knew she wouldn't see Alekos again. She was Cinderella minus a glass slipper, and soon she'd be left in rags with a pumpkin for a carriage. *And Lukas for a husband.* She suppressed a shudder at the thought.

Lukas checked his phone, frowning. 'Your father needs me in a meeting.'

'A meeting at two in the morning?' Iolanthe knew she

shouldn't be surprised. Her father had always worked long hours. He often stayed in Athens for months at a time, returning to his country estate only for the most cursory of visits.

'I'll be back shortly,' Lukas told her. 'You should wait inside.'

Disheartened beyond all measure, Iolanthe watched Lukas stride away before she turned back to the hotel's opulent lobby. With her feet aching in her new shoes and her body throbbing disconsolately from the memory of Alekos's touch, she felt more alone than she had in a long while. More lonely, and with nothing to look forward to.

She was about to sink into one of the elegant armchairs gracing the marble-floored space when her whole body stiffened with awareness, every sense coming exquisitely alive as Alekos walked out of the hotel's bar.

She started towards him instinctively, one hand outstretched, her sense of loneliness evaporating in the sudden, demanding need to see him, speak to him, *touch* him—

Iolanthe didn't care how reckless or desperate she seemed to him or anyone else. She had waited her whole life, and in that moment she was sure it had been for this. For a future that didn't look like a prison cell, a possibility of excitement and adventure. For Alekos.

Alekos had spent the last two hours drinking steadily in the hotel's bar. So much so that while he wasn't precisely drunk, he questioned the vision of loveliness in front of him, thinking he must have imagined Iolanthe into being. He'd certainly been thinking about her enough, though he'd tried not to.

He'd watched from the edge of the ballroom as she'd danced with that wet blanket of a keeper, a man who seemed ill at ease in his own body, shuffling his feet and holding Iolanthe awkwardly.

Then when Alekos could bear no more he'd headed for the bar. He couldn't stand seeing Iolanthe with anyone, even someone as unthreatening as her buffoonish dance partner. He couldn't shake the deep-seated feeling that she was *his*, that no one else could touch her. He'd been her first kiss, and he wanted to be even more. Somehow Iolanthe, this innocent sprite, had branded herself on his soul, reminded him of what he'd once been like, what life was like when you held on to happiness and hope. When you believed good things could happen.

And now she was here, real and alive, her face suffused with happiness at the mere sight of him.

'Alekos...' Iolanthe whispered, her mouth curving into a smile of pure joy as she reached out one hand to touch him.

Alekos responded instinctively to her unhidden response, even as he acknowledged that she made no sense. He was a stranger who wanted her body. Didn't she realise that? Didn't she understand how dangerous he was to her well-being?

Alekos wrapped his hand around hers to keep her from touching him, and realised instantly that he'd made a mistake. Instead of pushing her away, he merely pulled her closer, finding it impossible to resist her enchanting allure.

'I thought you'd left.' His voice came out low and gravelly, harsh with wanting.

'No, not yet.' She spoke in a breathless whisper, her eyes shining. 'I'm so happy to see you again.'

Briefly Alekos closed his eyes. Iolanthe had no idea what such heartfelt honesty *did* to him. 'Iolanthe...'

'When I didn't see you at the ball, I thought you'd tired of me.' She nibbled her lip, appalled realisation swamping her eyes. 'That is, you haven't, have you...?'

'No. I haven't.' Although God knew he should have. She was inexperienced, innocent, *dull*. For both their sakes she had to be. The alternative was breaking her heart and shattering her naïve hopes as he took what he so desperately craved from her and then walked away as he knew he would. As he had to. He took a deep breath. 'I was just about to go upstairs.'

'Upstairs?'

'I have a suite at the hotel.' For the last four years he'd been living in Corinth, close to his factory and warehouses, making sure security was tight and all technical information highly classified. He would not have an invention stolen from him a second time. Taking a suite for the evening of the ball had been expedient.

'You do?' Her eyes widened and Alekos saw the suggestion in them as clearly as if she'd verbalised it. And he realised, to his own shame, that he'd mentioned the suite because he wanted her there. Of course he did.

'You could come up for a drink,' he said gruffly, well aware he was plunging down a road he had no business to tread for a single step. One drink. A kiss or two. And then he would let her go. For ever.

'All right,' she agreed shyly, and Alekos wondered if she even knew what she was getting into...or if he did.

Iolanthe spared no more than a fleeting thought for Lukas and her father before stepping into the lift with Alekos. Maybe she was being foolish, even stupid. And if not that, then reckless and wanton. Right then she didn't care. This felt like her only chance at happiness. She and Alekos had a connection; even he acknowledged it.

If she didn't go with him now, the prison doors would close for ever.

Tonight was for magic.

Alekos ushered her out of the lift and down a long, plushly carpeted hall, before he swiped his key card at the door at the end, and then swung the door open to reveal a luxurious suite with floor-to-ceiling views of the Acropolis.

Iolanthe's breath came out in a rush as she stepped into the open-plan living area of the elegant space, barely noticing the leather sofas and ebony and teak coffee tables as awareness rippled over her skin and alarm twisted in her stomach.

What was she doing here?

'A drink,' Alekos said, and went to the minibar tucked in a corner of the room. Iolanthe dropped her bag and mask on a nearby sofa, unease and excitement warring within her. This was dangerous, crazy—and also incredibly exciting. Common sense told her she should bolt, and yet she stayed put. She couldn't bear the thought of the evening ending, the doors slamming shut on her future. And she wanted Alekos to kiss her again.

Alekos took a bottle of champagne from the little fridge and held it out to her. 'Seems appropriate, don't you think?'

'I suppose.' She'd only tasted champagne a few times in her life.

Alekos popped the cork, the sound a mini explosion in the stillness of the room, and then poured them each a flute. He handed one to Iolanthe and she took it with numb fingers. *'Gia sou.'*

'Gia sou,' she whispered, and drank. The bubbles fizzed up her nose, making her cough. Alekos arched an eyebrow and Iolanthe tried for a laugh. 'Sorry. I never seem to get the hang of champagne.'

'Innocent in this as in everything else.'

Something about his tone made her prickle defensively. 'I can't help being innocent.'

'Well I know it.'

She cocked her head, noting the way his eyes had narrowed and his mouth had firmed. Did he not want her here? Did he regret asking her up? She couldn't bear the thought. 'What is it?' she asked unsteadily. 'Why are you looking at me like that?'

'Because you shouldn't be here,' Alekos said, the words

harsh and unrelenting, confirming her fears. 'I shouldn't have asked you up here. You don't know what you're getting into, Iolanthe.'

A thrill ran through her, and to her surprise Iolanthe recognised it as excitement rather than fear. 'What if I do know?' she dared to ask.

Alekos took a step closer to her. 'Do you?' he returned, his voice low; Iolanthe couldn't tell if his words were a threat or an invitation. Maybe both.

And the truth was, she didn't know. At least she recognised that much. She knew what happened between men and women, she understood the basics of sex, but *this*... desire was utterly new to her. And completely intoxicating. She couldn't leave. Not now, not when Alekos was offering such a tantalising glimpse of a new world, a world she'd only dreamed of and read about in books. She'd wanted a kiss, but even she in her innocence recognised the look of blatant intent in Alekos's eyes, and knew he was thinking of far more than a kiss.

And what of it? The rest of her life would be one shackled to duty. Why not allow herself one night of pleasure— and maybe it could become more? Maybe, she thought with sudden, dizzying hope, Alekos could be a suitable husband for her. Why not?

Why shouldn't this be the beginning of everything?

She met his hot gaze, if not fearlessly, then at least with determination. With desire. And she shuddered when he reached his hand out and stroked her cheek.

'So soft,' he murmured. He looked as dazed as she felt. He wanted this as much as she did. The realisation was both thrilling and terrifying, and Iolanthe met it full on. Here was her future. Her hope.

'Kiss me,' she whispered.

Alekos hesitated, and through the fog of her desire Iolanthe saw the conflict on his face, felt it in the way his fingers stilled on her cheek.

'It doesn't matter if I'm innocent,' she said fiercely. 'I don't want to be innocent or naïve. I want to feel and taste and *know*. I want to be desired.'

'You are,' Alekos assured her raggedly, and then he drew her towards him, their bodies colliding in sweet harmony as his mouth came down on hers.

Iolanthe revelled in the touch of his lips against hers, everything in her jolting alive as his tongue swept into her mouth and his hands roved her body, leaving fire and longing in their wake. His palm cupped her breast and it felt as if he'd hotwired her soul. She'd never known you could feel like this. *Want* like this...

She clutched his shoulders, and then dared to smooth her hands down his shirt, her palms caressing the sculpted muscles beneath the crisp cotton. Alekos let out a groan as he tore his mouth from hers.

'Iolanthe, you should leave now,' he urged on a ragged gasp.

Leave now, when her senses were swimming and her body ached for his touch? When she felt as if everything was finally *beginning*? That was the last thing she wanted. She knew she was plunging down a road where there was no way back, but she didn't *want* a way back. She wanted to dare to go ahead...with Alekos.

'Let me stay,' she whispered, and pressed her palms against his chest so she could feel the hard thud of his heart. 'Please.'

His eyes glittered gold as he gazed down at her, his breathing coming in ragged bursts. 'Do you realise what you're asking?' he demanded in a low voice.

A smile curved her mouth even as her heart lurched. 'I'm not that innocent.' *Not quite.* If Alekos took her innocence, she'd be ruined for another man. She knew that, at least in her head, but her heart was hammering with an insistence that this was right. This was her chance, and she *had* to take it.

'We can't...' Alekos began, but Iolanthe thought he was waiting to be convinced. And so she would convince him.

'We can.' Standing on her tiptoes, she brushed her mouth against his, a butterfly kiss that had Alekos shuddering in response—and then kissing her back, his hands sliding to her hips to anchor her against his arousal as his tongue delved deep.

Iolanthe rocked against his hips, thrilling to his touch, to the knowledge that he desired her so powerfully. Her mind was a haze of need and sensation, and she quieted the distant voice that was telling her to stop, to see sense, to realise this could only be a mistake. She and Alekos had a connection, something precious and rare. Never mind that they'd only known each other a few hours. She felt it, and she knew he felt it as well.

'If you're sure,' Alekos muttered, and in reply Iolanthe pressed herself closer still.

Alekos couldn't think beyond the feel of Iolanthe's slender body against his own. He felt as if she'd slipped into his senses; he couldn't remember ever wanting a woman this way. So much so that all rational thought and self-control fled and his hands shook as he tugged at the zip on the back of her dress.

The sparkly satin, as white as a wedding dress, fell away to reveal her pale and perfect body underneath. Alekos released the breath he'd been holding in a low, slow exhalation as his gaze roved over her.

'You are exquisite.'

Pink stained her cheeks but she did not try to hide herself. Her small, high breasts were encased in delicately scalloped lace, and the scrap of silk that passed for a pair of pants was transparent enough for him to see the soft darkness beneath. Everything in him longed to touch her.

Alekos took her hand and Iolanthe stepped out of the

dress, the satin whispering about her slender legs. Her hands went to his chest, fingers fumbling on the studs of his shirt, her lovely brow puckered in concentration. With an impatient hiss of breath Alekos pulled them out himself and then shrugged out of the shirt, tossing his cummerbund aside.

Iolanthe's mouth curved and her eyes glowed as she stroked his bare chest, her fingers teasing the crisp hair. '*You're* exquisite,' she said, and he laughed, the sound hoarse.

'No one has ever called me that before.'

'They should.' With soft hands she stroked his chest and torso, down to the waistband of his trousers where she stopped shyly. 'You're beautiful, Alekos.'

'Come to bed.' Even through the fog of his desire Alekos saw the flicker of uncertainty in her eyes but then she came willingly, proudly even, her chin held high as she walked towards him, her hips swaying.

He should stop this. He knew he should stop this, before Iolanthe got hurt, before he was the one who hurt her. Then she lifted silvery eyes to his face, her whole expression one of acceptance and invitation and *hope*, and, with a suppressed groan, he took her hand and led her towards the bedroom.

The silken sheets were slippery and cool under Iolanthe's naked body. Within seconds Alekos joined her on the bed, taking her into his arms. Somehow he'd become naked. She felt the hard muscles of his chest, the rough hair of his legs, and, most excitingly, the insistent throb of his erection, all against her. It was almost too much sensation, short-circuiting her thought processes, so all she could do was feel and respond.

Iolanthe arched against him, sucking in a shocked breath as his hands skimmed her most private places. No one had ever touched her so intimately, and then more intimately still as Alekos's hand stroked between her legs and pleasure flared.

'You like that?' he murmured huskily.

'Yes.' She buried her head in his neck, embarrassed by her own overwhelming reaction. Alekos continued to touch her with such sure expertise that it wasn't long before her body was acting of its own accord, legs parting, hips thrusting as she sought the apex of the pleasure he gave her.

She'd only just reached that shining pinnacle, her body shuddering with the force of a climax that shocked her with its intensity, when Alekos was poised over her, his arousal nudging her thighs, his face drawn into harsh lines and angles.

'Iolanthe...'

'Yes.' She arched upwards, accepting him into her body, craving him all the more. Even so, that first tender invasion made her gasp, her body stiffening against the unfamiliar sensation.

Alekos stilled, his breath coming in tearing gasps as he waited for her to adjust to the feel of him. 'Is this—?'

'It's fine.' She breathed in deeply, letting the sense of completeness flood her senses. 'It's good.' And it was good, wonderful even, as she reeled at the newness and strangeness of it, understanding instinctively that she had crossed a threshold and could never go back. She was innocent no longer.

Then Alekos began to move inside her and thoughts fled her mind as she matched his rhythm, pleasure beginning to build once more, higher and higher, until she was crying out as she clutched his shoulders.

Alekos let out a groan as his body shuddered inside her, his head buried in the curve of her neck as Iolanthe closed her eyes and gave herself up to pleasure.

* * *

Alekos rolled off her, one arm thrown across his face as the last of his climax shuddered through him.

What had he done?

What had he been thinking, taking Iolanthe's virginity? He hadn't even used birth control. All he could think was that some sort of madness had gripped him, holding him in its thrall all evening. And now that his body was finally sated, his mind acknowledged the disastrous consequences of his actions, and regret and remorse replaced the lust that had overwhelmed him so utterly.

He'd taken something from her he'd had no right to take, no matter that they'd both been compliant, eager even. He bore the responsibility, the blame.

Alekos lowered his arm and glanced at Iolanthe. She lay on her back, her face flushed, a damp tendril of ink-black hair curling against her cheek. Her eyes were closed, but they fluttered open as if she sensed his scrutiny, and her hesitant gaze clashed with his as she bit her lip.

'I'm sorry,' Alekos said in a low voice. Iolanthe flinched.

'Sorry?' she repeated, her voice wobbling. 'Why?'

Alekos heaved a sigh. 'I shouldn't have done this. It was my fault entirely.'

Her eyes flashed. 'Did I have no say in it, then?'

Alekos smiled tiredly, heartened to see that she could show some spirit despite their situation. 'Perhaps, but you are young—'

'Stop telling me how *young* I am.' She scrambled up to a sitting position, reaching for the rumpled sheet to clutch to her chest. Her dark hair tumbled around her shoulders and, although her eyes still flashed, her lips trembled. 'I'm twenty.' Six years younger than him. Alekos felt a stab of pity mixed with shameful irritation. He didn't want her tears. 'I don't regret anything,' she said defiantly. 'Maybe we rushed things, but it doesn't change how I feel.'

Alekos stilled, his gaze narrowing as his insides iced. 'How you feel?' he repeated neutrally.

'Yes...' Iolanthe's fingers clenched on the sheet. 'We... we have a connection, Alekos.' She nodded towards the still-warm bed. 'Obviously.'

'A sexual connection,' he clarified flatly. Iolanthe frowned.

'Yes, but...it's more than that, surely?' Her teeth sank into her lip again as she gazed at him, and Alekos suppressed a groan at the uncertainty he saw there. The innocence and honesty that had mere hours ago intrigued and attracted him now only appalled.

He should have expected this. He *had* expected it, before he'd let his libido obliterate his brain. Iolanthe had confused sex with love. How could she have done otherwise, considering her inexperience?

The kindest thing, the only thing, to do was be blunt. Ruthless. Refuse to allow even the smallest bud of hope to be nurtured. Hope, he knew, was a cruel thing when it wasn't warranted. And it wasn't warranted with him.

Alekos rose from the bed and reached for his trousers, his back to her as he stated flatly, 'It's not more than that, Iolanthe. We desired one another physically. We had sex. That's it.' Each word felt like a grenade hurled into the room, ready to explode. From the bed Alekos heard an audible sniff and he closed his eyes, forcing back the acidic burn of regret. Another sniff.

Reaching for his shirt, Alekos turned to face Iolanthe. In the few seconds it had taken him to dress and turn around, she'd composed herself and now lifted her chin, her eyes giving away nothing save for a telltale sheen. She still clutched the sheet to her chest.

'I see.' She spoke with dignity, even if her voice wobbled, and Alekos felt a flicker of admiration for her strength of spirit. 'So that's it, then? You take my virginity and kick me to the door?'

'You offered it,' Alekos retorted before he could stop himself.

'And you take what's on offer, I suppose?' Her lovely face contorted with contempt that cut him to the quick. 'I'm really very stupid, aren't I? I thought...I thought...' She shook her head, self-disgust and sorrow evident on every line of her face.

Regret lashed at him, a painful scourge. 'I'm sorry.'

'I knew what I was doing.' She laughed, the sound harsh and high. 'I thought you might be a suitable husband, one my father would approve of. But the thought probably appals you, doesn't it?'

He found he couldn't bear her self-mockery. 'It doesn't appal me.'

'No? But you want me out of here as soon as possible. Inexperienced as I am, I recognise that much.'

'I...' Suddenly he felt flummoxed, unsure of what he wanted. He knew he didn't want to hurt this lovely young woman.

'Don't worry.' She cut across his floundering. 'Let me get dressed and then I'll go.'

'I'm sorry if I misled you,' Alekos said wretchedly. 'You are very beautiful, Iolanthe, and charming. I've been enchanted by you all evening, and I'm sure you will ensnare a man in no time—'

'Please spare me that pretty little speech,' Iolanthe cut him off, her voice cold and clear. 'I don't wish to *ensnare* anyone. I am not a spider.'

'Poor choice of words. I'm sorry.'

'You seem very apologetic tonight.' Iolanthe rose from the bed, the sheet wrapped around her, her cheeks flaring with colour.

'I am. I shouldn't have invited you up here, and I certainly shouldn't have taken you to bed.' Alekos took a deep breath. 'We didn't even use birth control.'

Iolanthe's eyes widened with panic for a single second

before her expression cleared. 'Even I know how unlikely a pregnancy is after just one time.'

'Yet still possible.'

Her fingers tightened on the sheet and she cocked her head, her narrowed gaze sweeping over him. 'So what would happen if I was pregnant?'

Alekos hesitated. 'I take my responsibilities seriously.'

'Which means?'

His mouth firmed into a hard line. 'We'll address that situation if it occurs.'

'How reassuring.' She stalked out of the bedroom, nearly tripping over the edge of the sheet, and Alekos watched her go, caught between frustration and regret. He still couldn't believe he'd lost control of himself so completely. What was it about her that had enflamed him so? Perhaps it had simply been a matter of needs must; he had not had a woman in his bed in months, thanks to his demanding work schedule. At this point he couldn't imagine what else it could have been.

He walked into the sitting room of the suite; Iolanthe's narrow back was to him as she struggled to fasten her bra.

'Let me help—'

'No.' Her voice shook and she took a deep breath. 'The kindest thing you can do is wait in the bedroom while I get myself out of here.' Another breath. 'Please.' She slipped into her dress, struggling to zip it up even halfway.

'I don't want to leave you like this.'

'But you want me to leave.'

For a second Alekos considered the alternative. Having her stay. Getting to know her. Marrying her, even. Then he thought of all the accompanying emotional risks and his heart shut that possibility right down. 'Iolanthe, please. Let me take you home, at least.'

'My father is waiting downstairs.' She let out a high, trembling laugh. 'And trust me, I don't want him to know where I've been.'

'Will you...will you be in trouble?' Alekos asked in a low voice. It was the twenty-first century, after all. How shameful was it for a twenty-year-old woman to have sex? A twenty-year-old virgin who had told him her father would arrange her marriage?

Alekos closed his eyes in guilty regret. What the hell had he been thinking? He owed Iolanthe more than this. 'Please, Iolanthe, let me help you.'

'How?' she demanded, and before Alekos could answer he heard voices from the hall and then, to his incredulous amazement, the door to the suite swung open. He blinked in stunned surprise at the sight of the man Iolanthe had been dancing with, and, behind him, Alekos's nemesis, Talos Petrakis.

'What the hell—?' Alekos began, but he didn't get a chance to say anything else for Petrakis's burly body-guards swarmed in and grabbed him, twisting his arms painfully behind his back.

'Papa!'

In stunned horror Alekos watched Iolanthe move to her father, her arms outstretched.

'Get behind me, Iolanthe,' Petrakis said in a low voice, but Alekos didn't hear what else the man said. *Papa?* Petrakis was Iolanthe's *father?*

'Deal with him,' Petrakis bit out with a nod towards Alekos. The bodyguards started hustling him towards the door. Alekos struggled against them and received a sharp elbow in his kidneys for his pains.

'I'm not a naïve university student any more,' he grated as he continued to struggle to resist the two men. 'You can't treat me like this, Petrakis—'

Petrakis did not spare him so much as a glance. 'Iolanthe,' he said, and he put his arm around his daughter. 'Come with me.'

The last thing Alekos saw was Iolanthe's pale face as her father shepherded her away.

CHAPTER THREE

'IT IS TIME to discuss your future.'

Talos Petrakis stared at his daughter from behind his desk, his expression terrifyingly blank, while Iolanthe flushed and looked away. 'Iolanthe? You cannot go on like this.'

'I know,' she whispered. It had been nearly a month since her father had found her with Alekos Demetriou, and what a horrible month it had been. She'd been virtually imprisoned in her room at their town house in Athens, and the few times she'd seen her father he'd been cold and contemptuous, disgust at her behaviour evident in every stern line of his face. And could she really blame him?

Even now, four weeks later, Iolanthe couldn't believe how rashly, how *stupidly* she'd acted. It had been as if Alekos Demetriou had cast some awful spell over her. To have sex with a stranger she'd only met hours before, thinking it would actually lead to something...!

It had been utter madness. Pleasurable madness, she remembered that all too well, but then she really had thought they'd been building some sort of future. In her naïvety she'd thought a sexual connection indicated an emotional one. The memory of how ruthlessly Alekos had dismantled that dream made Iolanthe inwardly cringe even now. Of course it had only been sex. She'd seen him as her chance of escape but he hadn't wanted it. Hadn't wanted her.

'Iolanthe?' Talos prompted coldly. 'You realise the desperate situation you are in, I hope.'

Iolanthe's startled gaze moved back to her father. 'Desperate?' she repeated warily. She'd spent the last month essentially quarantined, with only books and a sketchpad for company, while her father had gone about his business and barely spoken to her. His physical and emotional withdrawal had hurt her more than she'd thought possible, especially on the heels of Alekos's rejection. Her father had never been close to her but she realised now how she had always stood on the bedrock of his approval and love. Which made her actions on the night of the ball even more reprehensible and foolish.

'You are spoiled goods,' Talos stated. 'Damaged beyond repair. What man will have you now?'

Iolanthe flinched at her father's flat statement. His words belonged in another century, and yet she knew in his world—and hers—they held truth. 'Someone who loves me...' she managed in a hesitant whisper.

'And what man would love a woman who gave herself to a stranger so wantonly?' Talos shook his head, hurt flashing in his eyes. 'Truly, Iolanthe, I am still shocked. I did not think you capable of such an act of wanton disobedience.'

She clenched her hands together, knuckles aching. 'I made a mistake, Papa, I know that.'

'A mistake with terrible consequences,' Talos returned. He sighed, sitting back in his chair as he massaged his temples. 'Where did I go wrong, Iolanthe? That you would treat me this way?' Talos regarded her for a moment, his expression stony. 'You must marry,' he stated. 'Fortunately Lukas is willing to have you.'

'Even now?' Iolanthe said bitterly, and ire flashed across her father's face.

'You are fortunate he is willing to overlook your indiscretion.'

'Yes, of course.' So now she was *lucky* to have Lukas Callos. The realisation was bitter. She felt like a lame mare that had to be offloaded onto some charitable soul or else made into glue.

'Your other option,' Talos continued implacably, 'is to

remain shut up at my country villa, and remain a shame to my name. It is not what I would prefer.'

Iolanthe closed her eyes briefly. The prison doors were inexorably swinging shut.

'I will give you a day to think about it,' Talos said, with the air of someone who was granting a great favour. 'But no longer. I don't want Lukas to change his mind.'

But Lukas would most likely change his mind, Iolanthe thought, her heart like a stone inside her, when he learned just how mired in shame she was. It had been four weeks since her night with Alekos, and she hadn't had a period. The newfound queasiness in the mornings, the tenderness in her breasts, the overwhelming fatigue...all of it pointed to a truth she'd been doing her desperate best to ignore. She was pregnant. Lukas might be willing to marry her as spoiled goods, but would he take Alekos's bastard child as his own? And didn't Alekos deserve to know about his child?

'I will think about it, Papa,' Iolanthe promised woodenly, even though the prospect of pledging her life to Lukas Callos made everything in her sink in resignation and despair. But before she thought of Lukas, she needed to see Alekos. They'd parted terribly, yes, but he'd said he wanted to know about their child. And maybe, *maybe* he would soften towards her if he knew she carried his baby. Maybe he would be reminded of how much they had shared.

It was the stuff of romantic fantasy, she realised that, and yet Iolanthe clung to it all the same. What other hope did she have?

'Papa,' she said hesitantly. 'What about...what about Alekos Demetriou?'

Talos stilled, his eyebrows snapping together in displeasure. 'What about him?' he growled.

'Couldn't he...couldn't he be a suitable husband?'

Her father's face darkened, fury flashing in his eyes,

making Iolanthe take an instinctive step backwards. She'd never seen her father look so angry before. 'You have no idea about Demetriou,' Talos spat.

She swallowed hard, one hand pressed to her throat. 'What do you mean?'

'You think he cared for you, Iolanthe?' Talos demanded. 'He was using you, to get at me. He's always had it in for me, ever since I came out with a software system he was trying to develop himself. The trouble was Demetriou wasn't fast or smart enough to keep up. It set his company back years, and he's blamed me. You were no more than part of his petty revenge.'

Iolanthe stared at Talos in appalled realisation. Alekos had a history with her father? A bad history? 'No...' she whispered. 'That can't be—'

'I assure you,' Talos cut across her, 'it is.'

Iolanthe shook her head, wanting to deny such a terrible reality. 'But how did he even know I was your daughter?'

Talos shrugged. 'The man does his research. I'll give him that much.'

'But...' She remembered the way Alekos had held her as they'd danced, the brush of his fingers against her cheek. It hadn't *felt* like revenge. At least not until afterwards, when he hadn't seemed able to get her out of his bed, his life, fast enough.

Sickly Iolanthe recognised how unlikely it was that a man like Alekos would have sought her out with such determination. Would have seduced her with such thoroughness. He must have had an ulterior motive, and it seemed that it was revenge. The realisation was bitter indeed, making what had happened between them seem even more sordid. 'I can't believe it,' she said numbly, even though she already did.

'Believe it,' Talos returned flatly. 'And marry Lukas Callos.'

* * *

Alekos stared at the announcement in yesterday's *Athinapoli* and told himself he felt nothing. So Iolanthe was marrying Lukas Callos, her dull keeper from the ball. Was he really surprised? She'd told him herself that her father would arrange her marriage. Her father... *Talos Petrakis.*

Bitterness surged through him at the memory of the last time he'd come face-to-face with his enemy. After bursting into his hotel suite, Petrakis's thugs had taken him to an alley behind the hotel and beaten him almost senseless. It infuriated him even now to think that Petrakis would flout the law with such easy indifference. To have a grown man, an upstanding member of the business community, beaten as if he were some nameless street rat. The fact that Alekos had at one time been hardly distinguishable from a street rat only made him more determined to avenge himself on Petrakis. Nothing would stop him now. Nothing—and no one—would sway him from his purpose, even for an instant.

As for Iolanthe Petrakis... Alekos's mouth firmed into an unforgiving line. Who knew what had been in that pretty head of hers? Perhaps she'd set him up, fully intending for her father to find them together. How else would Petrakis have known where she was? Where *he* was?

She'd certainly pressed herself on him. Looking back, Alekos could only wonder at Iolanthe's determined urgency to lose her virginity to a stranger. Perhaps she'd wanted to rebel against her father and the strict isolation he'd kept her in. Perhaps she hadn't realised how overwhelming it had all become. In any case it didn't matter whether she'd been conniving or merely naïve. He couldn't trust her. He wouldn't trust anyone.

'There's a woman here to see you,' Stefanos, his bodyguard, said as he appeared in the doorway of Alekos's study. Alekos had hired Stefanos after Petrakis's attack; he intended never to be caught like that again.

Now Alekos stiffened in surprise. No one visited him at home; the apartment in Athens' Plaka district that he'd recently rented was private, the address unlisted. 'Did she give a name?'

'Just a first name. Iolanthe.' Stefanos's face was impassive as he waited for Alekos's orders.

Alekos tossed the newspaper onto a nearby table and drove a hand through his hair. How had Iolanthe found him here? Clearly she was more resourceful than he'd realised. And why did she want to see him? To gloat about her engagement? Or to tell him something else? He still felt uneasy about not having used birth control. For that reason only he would see her.

'Where is she?'

'I've left her waiting in the hall.'

'Put her in the drawing room,' Alekos commanded. 'I'll see her in a moment.'

Stefanos nodded and withdrew from the room. Alekos rose from his chair and paced the confines of his study; despite cloaking himself in icy numbness for the last month, he felt an unwelcome welter of emotions at the prospect of seeing Iolanthe again. He had no idea what to think, to believe, of her any longer. She'd enchanted him once, but now he suspected he'd merely been duped, just as her father had once duped him, encouraging his ideas, clapping him on the shoulder, asking him to explain everything. Only twenty-two years old, Alekos had thought he'd found his mentor. His home. How wrong, how stupid he'd been. How trusting.

Never again, he vowed. Never would he trust a Petrakis, or anyone, again. Taking a deep breath, he squared his shoulders and strode from the room.

Iolanthe stared out at the dusky night framed by the curtains of Alekos's drawing-room window and tried to still the wild beating of her heart. She couldn't quite believe she'd possessed the audacity to slip out of her father's house and dart through the narrow streets of Athens' old district like some errant shadow. If her father discovered her here...

But she had to see Alekos. She had to know if he'd been using her as Talos had said. *And if he hadn't*...even now a girlish fantasy spun through her mind in shining, golden threads, of Alekos explaining everything, of her telling him about her pregnancy. He'd whisk her away and she wouldn't have to marry Lukas Callos. They'd live happily ever after, the end.

The door opened and Iolanthe whirled around, one hand pressed to her heart. Alekos stood in the doorway, *loomed* there, looking as darkly attractive as ever, and also utterly unwelcoming. The mouth that had kissed her so thoroughly was now thinned into an uncompromising line, and eyes that had glittered gold with desire now looked flat and hard. The straight slashes of his dark eyebrows were drawn together in a frown as he folded his arms across his impressive chest and stared at her in silent hostility.

Those golden threads of fantastical possibility disintegrated in an instant. What was she doing here? Why had she come? Iolanthe swallowed, and then started to speak.

'Alekos...'

'How did you find me?'

She jerked back at the aggression in his voice. 'Your address was among my father's papers.' She'd sneaked into Talos's study late one evening, surprised but gratified to find Alekos Demetriou's details on his desk. No doubt her father wanted to know more about the man who had ruined his daughter. Except in reality she'd ruined herself, by being so phenomenally stupid.

'Ah.' Alekos nodded, unsurprised, unimpressed. 'What do you want?' There was no welcome in the words, no warmth or even negligible interest. Of course not. Every damning word her father had spoken had its proof in this moment.

'I wanted to see you,' Iolanthe said in a low voice. 'I wanted to know if...if...'

'If what?'

She stared at him miserably, fully aware of how foolish and pointless this mission had been. It had been one last desperate act before the noose tightened around her neck. 'If there was anything real between us,' she whispered, the words like bile in her mouth. She knew now there wasn't.

And as for their child? Could she really tell him about their pregnancy now? Even if Alekos agreed to marry her, Iolanthe didn't know if she could stand a union based on convenience and built on the foundations of hatred.

'Anything real?' Alekos repeated incredulously. 'You can actually ask that, after your father burst into my hotel and dragged me away like some thug?'

Iolanthe stared at him, her eyes wide. 'He...he was protecting me.'

'And you're defending him.' His unyielding gaze raked over her, dismissing her in an instant. 'Get out, Iolanthe. I don't want to see you again. Ever.' His eyes glittered, but with malice rather than the desire she'd once thrilled to see there. 'Unless there were consequences?'

Iolanthe stared at him, appalled and more than a little frightened by the anger she saw in his eyes, felt in his taut body. It radiated out from him, a malevolent force.

'Well?' he demanded. 'Are you here because you are carrying my child? Because if it is for any other reason, then I advise you to leave. Immediately.'

Iolanthe tasted the acid sting of bile in the back of her throat. His words sounded and felt like a threat. How could she tell him she was pregnant now? Was this cold, forbidding man, a man bent on some kind of sick revenge, the one she wanted as the father of her child?

And yet even now Alekos surely had a right to know.

'What would you do, if there were consequences?' she whispered.

'Hedging your bets?' Alekos scoffed. 'I saw the announcement that you were marrying Callos.' His gaze darkened and he reached for her, one powerful hand encircling her wrist. 'Don't lie to me, Iolanthe. Are you pregnant?'

His fingers felt like a vice on her arm. Terror clawed at her insides. Where was the gentle, funny, charming man she'd fallen for? Evaporated, like the mirage he'd been all along.

'No,' she managed to get out of her too-tight throat. 'No, I'm not pregnant.'

Alekos released her, contempt twisting his mouth. 'Fine,' he said. 'Then leave.'

Iolanthe blinked back useless tears. She would *not* cry now. Not in front of this cold, hard stranger.

Alekos waited, his arms folded, saying nothing, impatience radiating from him. Iolanthe drew a ragged breath and then, swallowing the sob that threatened to escape, she turned on her heel and fled.

Outside, the air was warm and sultry, the stars like diamond pinpricks in the black velvet drop cloth of the sky. Iolanthe tipped her head to stare up at the sky and willed the tears back. No more tears, not ever again. She'd grown up tonight. She'd truly put her childish ways behind her, for better or for worse, and she would not go back to them.

She drew a deep breath and squared her shoulders, and then began the long walk back to her father's villa. Hopefully no one would have noticed that she'd gone; she'd told the housekeeper, Amara, that she was going to bed early, and then slipped out when her father had been enclosed in his study.

In the Plaka, people were filling up the bars and cafés, and amidst the mingled laughter and chat Iolanthe heard the strains of *rebetiko*, the folk music popular in such establishments. All the sounds and sights combined together to form a picture of carefree happiness that felt a million miles from her reality.

Iolanthe knew she had no choice now. Alekos Demetriou's attitude had made that clear to her. She was pregnant, dependent on her father's charity, without friend or resource, damaged and desperate.

She would marry Lukas Callos.

Two weeks later Alekos saw the marriage announcement in the *Athinapoli*.

Heiress Iolanthe Petrakis marries Petra Innovation's Lukas Callos.

There was a photo; Iolanthe looked lovely, if pale, in a sheath dress of off-white. She clutched a posy of lilies; Callos's face was bland, almost indifferent. It had been a small affair.

Acid churning in his gut, Alekos tossed the newspaper away and vowed never to think of Iolanthe Callos again. All he would let himself think about was success—and revenge.

CHAPTER FOUR

Ten years later

'I'M SORRY TO say your position is…difficult.'

'Difficult?' Iolanthe straightened in the club chair that her husband's solicitor, Antonis Metaxas, had ushered her into moments ago to discuss Lukas's financial position. Her husband of nearly a decade had died in a car accident a fortnight ago, leaving Iolanthe alone in the world save for her nine-year-old son Niko. Her father had died two years earlier, and Petra Innovation now belonged to her— and was Niko's legacy.

Metaxas steepled his fingers together, his expression a little too compassionate. The nape of Iolanthe's neck prickled with alarm. She hadn't involved herself in her father and husband's business these last ten years; she hadn't been asked to. She'd focused on her son instead, on nurturing and protecting him, and on trying to be happy, or at least content with the way her life had turned out, a loveless marriage to a near stranger and a son she adored. It could have been worse.

Even as she'd carved out a life for herself, virtually separate from Lukas, she'd always thought she'd have Petra Innovation, for Niko's sake. Niko was the only heir of both Talos Petrakis and Lukas Callos. The company was his birthright.

'Petra Innovation has had some financial setbacks in recent years,' Metaxas explained carefully. 'I'm afraid it leaves you in a rather precarious position.'

Iolanthe's nails dug into her palms as she clutched her hands tightly together in her lap and took several even breaths. This was news she really did not need. 'Why don't you speak plainly, Kyrie Metaxas? How precarious *is* my position?' She lifted her chin and met the solicitor's gaze firmly. 'Is Petra Innovation solvent?'

'Solvent, yes.' He hesitated, his grandfatherly face pulled into a reluctant frown that made Iolanthe battle both impatience and anxiety.

'I can handle whatever it is you're going to tell me,' she informed the older man crisply, although in truth she didn't know if she could. At least she would try. 'What is it?'

'I fear your husband was not as financially savvy as your father,' Metaxas explained. 'He was a genius when it came to technical innovation, of course,' he added quickly.

'Yes, I know.' Lukas had spent far more time at work than he had at home. His first and only love had been computers, and Iolanthe had long ago accepted it. Long ago stopped looking or hoping for love or even affection. How could she, when she had never loved him back? Their marriage had been nothing but a convenient match of expediency, on both sides.

Now she met Metaxas's gaze directly. 'So what has happened to the company since Lukas took over after my father's death?'

'Six months ago he offered the company's shares on the open market. Your father had always been reluctant to take such a step, wanting complete control.'

Which sounded very much like her father. Iolanthe knew that Talos and Lukas had split the shares of the company. Or they had, until…

'So other people could then buy shares in Petra Innovation?'

'Yes—'

'But Lukas still maintained a controlling interest.' She knew enough about business, about *life*, to understand how important that was.

Metaxas sighed and shook his head. 'I'm afraid not.'

'What?' She blinked at him, shocked even now that her husband could have been so foolish. So stupid. 'So now that I have inherited Petra Innovation…how much of it do I actually have?'

'You have roughly forty per cent.'

'All right.' She took a deep breath, forced her thoughts to calm. 'That still must be a majority. The other sixty per cent of shares will be owned by many different people, surely—'

'No,' Metaxas contradicted her, his voice gentle. 'The other sixty per cent is now owned by one person. Your husband didn't realise it—the investments were made quietly, slyly even, under different corporate names, over the last few months. But the man at the source was the same.'

Iolanthe stared at him, her hands clutched together so tightly her nails were making half-moon marks in her palms. 'And who is this man?'

'Another tech wizard. Alekos Demetriou.'

She drew her breath in sharply, her nails digging in even deeper, but other than that gave away no reaction. In truth she was so stunned she didn't know how to react. *Alekos Demetriou.* She had schooled herself not to think of him these last long ten years. Tried to pretend he was not Niko's father, that his name meant nothing to her. All of it lies. All it had taken was for Metaxas to say his name to have her hurtling back to that wonderful, terrible night, when she'd known both pleasure and pain so acutely.

And now Alekos Demetriou owned her father's company? *Her* company? Except of course it wasn't hers at all.

'What does this mean exactly?'

'I don't know,' the older man admitted. 'Demetriou only just revealed that he has a controlling interest. I requested a meeting with him to discuss the future of the company.'

Iolanthe's stomach soured. 'So the future of Petra Innovation is up to Alekos Demetriou?'

'In a word, yes.'

Abruptly she rose from her seat and paced the room, stopping in front of the window that overlooked Athens' business district. She barely saw the wide boulevard, the neat buildings, busy people going to and fro. In her mind's eye she saw Alekos as she'd last seen him, in his own drawing room, his face cold and closed and forbidding, as he'd demanded she leave.

And so she had.

'Kyria Callos, I realise this news comes as a shock.'

'You have no idea,' Iolanthe admitted with a harsh laugh. What would Alekos do with the company? With her son's—*his* son's—inheritance? 'Do you think it likely that he will simply allow things to continue as they are?' Even as she spoke the question she knew it was a ridiculous hope. A naïve one, and she'd put naïvety behind her long ago. She'd had to. She knew how bent on revenge Alekos had been back then. A decade didn't seem to have changed things. He still wanted to get back at her father, her family, or maybe even her. Why else would he have bought controlling shares?

'I really don't know what Demetriou will do,' Metaxas answered. 'I don't know why he has essentially initiated a takeover of Petra Innovation. But the fact that he was secretive about it concerns me, of course.'

Iolanthe nodded numbly, her unseeing gaze still on the city street.

Metaxas cleared his throat. 'Do you have any history with Demetriou?' he asked.

'Me?' Iolanthe turned around, her expression once more composed, closed. 'What are you asking? I married Lukas when I was twenty.'

'Of course, of course, forgive me. I only meant, perhaps, between the families...' Metaxas trailed off as Iolanthe regarded him coolly, giving nothing away. She hoped.

'Demetriou was in a race with my father a long time

ago,' she said. 'Something about a software system. My father beat him to the invention—I think Demetriou was angry about it.' So angry that he'd seduced his daughter, all for a petty, pointless revenge.

'So you think he has bought the company as some sort of payback?'

'It seems like him.'

'You know him, then.'

'I know his deeds,' Iolanthe corrected crisply. 'And what my father told me. He is not an admirable man in any shape or form.' That she knew all too well.

Metaxas sighed heavily. 'This doesn't bode well for Petra Innovation. But I expect Demetriou will inform us of his plans when I meet him tomorrow.'

Iolanthe tensed, shock like an icy flame rippling through her body. 'He agreed to a meeting?'

'Yes—'

'With you,' Iolanthe said, repeating his words. Metaxas, like her husband and father before him, intended to cut her out of any business decisions. Before Lukas's death she'd made herself be content to stay at home, out of the way. But not any longer. Not when her son's inheritance was at stake. 'I want to be present at that meeting.'

Metaxas looked startled. 'If that is your wish,' he said after a pause. 'But as you know it had always been your husband's desire for you not to be bothered by business concerns—'

'And look where that got us,' Iolanthe finished. The thought of coming face-to-face with Alekos Demetriou again filled her with both terror and dread, but she would still do it. She wanted to know exactly what Alekos intended for her father's company—and for her son.

'Kyrie Metaxas and Kyria Callos will see you now.'

Alekos's mouth twisted in wry bitterness as he strode into the CEO's office at Petra Innovation. He might have been kept waiting like a supplicant, but he was one no longer, neither lackey nor slave. Petra Innovation, to all intents and purposes, belonged to him. And he found he was looking forward to informing Iolanthe Callos of that fact.

The receptionist opened the doors and he stalked through them, stopping abruptly at the sight of Iolanthe standing by the window, the sunlight gilding her dark hair. Looking upon her after so many years felt like a punch to the solar plexus, and he found, to his surprise and irritation, that he was suddenly breathless. Memories assaulted him, a kaleidoscope of images and sensations that he'd long ago determined to forget. A white silk mask, the petal-pink curve of a smooth cheek. The touch of her lips, the breathy sigh of her pleasure.

Resolutely he moved his gaze from the woman by the window to the other occupant of the room: her solicitor, Antonis Metaxas. Alekos gave one brief nod.

'Kyrie Metaxas.'

'Kyrie Demetriou.'

The silence stretched between the three of them, taut and brittle. Alekos glanced at Iolanthe again, determined not to react to her as he had before. At that first burning glance he'd thought she looked the same, but now he saw that she was older, just as he was. He glimpsed faint lines by her eyes, and, although she looked pale, he saw a composure to her that had not been there before. She was thirty years old and recently a widow. He noticed she wore a pale grey suit, a suitable colour for mourning. The jacket was belted around her slender waist and the pencil skirt emphasised her lithe figure. Her hair was caught up in a neat chignon and it made him remember how those inky locks had felt tumbling through his hands as he'd drawn her towards him for a deep kiss...

'Kyria Callos. May I offer my condolences on the recent loss of your husband?' He would observe the niceties.

Iolanthe inclined her head in regal acceptance of his

words. She didn't speak. Her face looked as if it had been made of marble, as blank as a statue, no expression visible in those mist-silver eyes.

'I have informed Kyria Callos of your controlling interest in the company,' Metaxas said. 'She would like to know what your intentions are regarding Petra Innovation.'

Alekos's gaze snapped to Metaxas. 'And can Kyria Callos speak for herself?' he asked with deliberate mildness. He moved his gaze back to Iolanthe, surprised and strangely gratified to see a flash of ire in her eye; the statue was gone.

'Yes, Kyria Callos can,' she informed him shortly. The sound of her voice was another surprise; gone was the girlish lilt, replaced by the crisp tones of a grown-up woman in control of her life, if not her business.

'Very well.' Alekos gave her a nod, just as she had given him. 'What is it you wish to know?'

'I wish to know why you have bought controlling shares in my father and husband's company,' she said, and he heard the dislike in her voice, mixed with contempt. The realisation that she scorned him made his resolve for revenge harden inside him, a core of steel that had been the basis of every choice and desire for his entire adult life. 'And were so secretive about it,' she added, tossing the words like an insult.

'If you had cared to dig a little deeper, you would have found that I was not as secretive about my purchases as you seem to think. It was simply that your husband did not care to look closely into the matter.'

A small gasp escaped her before she pressed her lips together. 'How dare you?'

'How dare I?' Alekos arched an eyebrow, coldly incredulous. Her fake posturing of outrage and hauteur he could handle; this he could dismiss. 'I did not realise I was daring anything at all. I was merely stating a fact. Your husband was desperate, Kyria Callos.'

'At least he was honourable,' Iolanthe shot back before she drew in a quick breath and composed herself. 'Something you've never been.'

'Kyria Callos—' Metaxas began, clearly shocked by this unprecedented exchange.

'Iolanthe and I have some history,' Alekos informed the solicitor with curt politeness. 'As you have most likely surmised.' He glanced back at Iolanthe; her eyes looked like lambent silver, shining with suppressed fury—and remembrance. Was she recalling, as he was, how explosive they'd been together? Ten years on and he still remembered how she'd felt and tasted. How irresistible she'd been to him, so much so that he'd thrown caution and common sense to the wind in order to possess her.

Thank goodness he'd learned a little self-control in the last decade. Of course, he'd made sure never to cross paths with Iolanthe again.

Now Metaxas shot Iolanthe a troubled glance, but she said nothing. 'Kyria Callos is naturally concerned about the nature of your business dealings—'

'My actions towards Petra Innovation have been completely legal,' Alekos cut him off smoothly. 'Which is more than I can say for Talos Petrakis or Lukas Callos.'

Metaxas stiffened with affront. 'Are you implying something—?'

'Implying, no. Merely stating fact. Again.' Alekos moved his gaze to Iolanthe once more. She was pale with shock, but her eyes snapped with fury, her mouth compressed. She still had her spirit, then. Why did that thought please him? Nothing about Iolanthe Callos pleased or even interested him. He had not thought of her in ten years. At least, he had made himself not think of her.

'So after initiating a hostile takeover of my father's company, you cast aspersions on him and my husband's character?' Iolanthe shook her head, her features pinching with dislike. 'I suppose I should have expected nothing less from you. Next you will be insulting me as well.'

'As far as I can tell, you are the only one casting insults.'

'I really think this has gone far enough,' Metaxas intervened. 'Perhaps we can keep to discussing what Kyrie Demetriou intends for Petra Innovation—'

'Of course.' Colour flared in Iolanthe's pale cheeks, making her look even lovelier. She was like a tall, dark flame, standing so straight and proud, refusing to be cowed. Alekos felt an unsettling mix of pity and admiration. Even so, her courage wouldn't keep him from dealing the lethal blow he'd intended for so long. He only wished Talos Petrakis were alive to see and feel it.

'I am more than happy to inform you both of my intentions for Petra Innovation,' Alekos stated. He'd been responding emotionally to Iolanthe; it was time to stick to facts. To savour them, and the sweet revenge he'd now enjoy to the full, cold as it was. 'My intention for Petra Innovation is to close the company and liquidate all of its assets.' He glanced at Iolanthe, registering the lovely mouth that had dropped open in shock, the hands hanging slack and useless by her sides. 'Forty per cent should keep you in relative comfort, although I'm afraid the company is not performing nearly as well as it once was.' Not like when it had been flogging the software system he had designed. Tech wizard Callos might have been, but he had not ever been able to match Alekos's inventions. Just copy them.

'You can't,' Iolanthe whispered.

'I can,' Alekos informed her flatly. 'Indeed I have already begun the process.'

'You're going to fire all the employees—'

'Are you so concerned for those nameless faces, or is it your own position that worries you?' Alekos cut across her, a new fury firing his voice. He'd thought he'd put this anger far, far behind him. But now, seeing Iolanthe here, knowing she had profited from his inventions, his work and life's blood, all the while married to that leech Callos, sleeping in his bed—

Rage was not a strong enough word.

It had taken a while for him to realise that Lukas Callos was the technical genius behind Talos Petrakis's business savvy; to understand that Callos had been the one to copy his design, at Petrakis's behest, all those years ago. And Iolanthe had been sharing his bed, the pampered, spoiled wife.

'How dare you accuse me?' Iolanthe whispered, the words a breath of fury. '*You*, of all people—'

'Clearly you hold me in low regard,' Alekos drawled in a bored voice. 'But it is of little consequence. The liquidation will go forward immediately.'

'I think we should all take a moment to—' Metaxas began, but Iolanthe cut across him, taking a step towards Alekos, one slender hand balled into a useless fist.

'You can't. Petra Innovation belongs to me.'

He stared at her, unmoved. 'Not any more.'

'My whole life, my *son's* life—'

He'd heard she'd had a son by Callos. He'd never seen the boy, of course, and didn't even know his name. And what did he care of his enemy's birthright? His own had been taken from him when Petrakis had kissed him on both cheeks and then stolen his idea. His illusions had been ripped away first by the father, and then his daughter. He had none left.

'I hope you are both adaptable,' Alekos said coolly and Iolanthe let out a choked cry.

'When I first met you, I thought you were a good man. You have proved me wrong again and again.'

Alekos stamped down on the flicker of regret he felt, a tiny, unfortunate flame that he quickly quenched. 'Then perhaps you are a fool,' he said coldly. 'To believe something when the evidence proves otherwise. Or,' he suggested, iron entering his voice, 'perhaps you should question which is the good man and which is the bad in this scenario. Good day.' Not trusting himself to say any more, he nodded tersely to both Metaxas and Iolanthe before turning to leave the room.

CHAPTER FIVE

'How was it?'

Amara, Iolanthe's housekeeper and closest confidante for the last ten years, having cared for her since she was a child, met her at the doorway of the town house near the Plaka that she'd lived in since her marriage.

'Terrible.' Iolanthe only just managed to choke out the word. An hour after meeting Alekos and she was still caught between fury and fear.

Amara's face paled as she took Iolanthe's coat. 'Let me get you a warm drink.' Amara's solution for everything was a cup of Greek mountain tea, considered a panacea in the region of central Greece from which she came. Over the years Iolanthe had learned to like the herbal tea, made of ironwort and flavoured with honey and lemon.

'Thank you, Amara,' she said as she moved past the housekeeper to the kitchen, the heart of the house. 'But I'm afraid a cup of tea is not going to solve my problems now. Where is Niko?'

'Upstairs, on the computer.'

As he so often was. Her son spent most of his time either reading, playing with his electrical gadgets, or on the computer. People and social situations were a continual struggle, despite Iolanthe's determined and increasingly desperate attempts to have him socialise.

She sank into a chair at the kitchen table and pressed trembling fingers to her temple. She was shaken in more ways than she cared to admit by seeing Alekos again. Not just by his awful plans for the company, but by the sheer presence of the man himself. He was just as darkly and devastatingly attractive now as he'd been ten years ago, when he'd stolen both her heart and her innocence. Even more so, more forbidding, with no hint of a smile to curve that once mobile mouth, no promise of laughter to lighten those topaz eyes. He'd looked like an angry god from the old myths and legends, someone come down from the stars to wreak his vengeance. And he had. Oh, he had. How could she lose Petra Innovation?

Amara busied herself at the range, plucking the roots and stems of the ironwort plant she always kept in supply and boiling them in a little brass pot on the stovetop. 'What has happened?' she asked as she plucked a mug from the rack and squeezed lemon juice and honey into it. 'I thought you went to speak to the solicitor as a matter of course.'

'So did I.' Iolanthe leaned back in her chair and briefly closed her eyes. It felt like an age since she'd taken a taxi to Metaxas's office, blithely thinking he would simply number her assets. Instead he'd told her she might as well not have any.

'Well, then?' Amara asked, a touch of impatience adding to the anxiety in her voice. She'd been part of Iolanthe's household for her entire marriage. 'Tell me what has happened.'

'Alekos Demetriou has taken over Petra Innovation.' Amara's eyes widened with surprise. No one knew that Alekos was Niko's father, no one save her, her father, and Lukas. It had been an agreement they had made when Lukas had agreed to take Iolanthe as his wife. He would raise Niko as his own, and to the whole world they would present a happy, united front. Or at least try. In the end, Lukas had not tried very hard at all.

'And what does this Demetriou intend to do with it?' Amara asked.

Briefly Iolanthe told her. Amara listened in silence, setting the mug of hot, fragrant tea in front of Iolanthe before sitting across from her with her own cup.

'Very well,' she said when Iolanthe had finished. 'But

it is not so terrible, surely? Forty per cent should see you and Niko cared for, and you never had anything to do with the company.'

'The company is Niko's birthright,' Iolanthe returned with feeling. 'My father lived for that company, and so did Lukas.' She took a sip of tea, swallowing the honey-sweetened liquid along with her bitterness. 'Niko has always looked forward to being a part of it.' Talos had, in the last years of his life, mellowed in his disappointment and anger towards Iolanthe, and he'd sometimes taken Niko to work with him, shown him the inheritance that shimmered so promisingly. Lukas had always ignored his cuckoo son, and Iolanthe suspected that Niko cared so much about Petra Innovation because he wanted to impress the man he believed to be his father. Now Lukas was dead, and the company was all her son had. 'I can't give it up without a fight. For Niko's sake I need to try.' She glanced up at Amara, forcing back the threat of tears. 'You know what it means to him.'

Amara sighed. 'Yes, but he is only nine.'

'All he has ever wanted is to work for Petra Innovation,' Iolanthe answered. 'To make his father and grandfather proud.' The tears she had blinked back now thickened in her throat. Niko had so many struggles, and only one hope. How could she take it from him?

'And if you have no choice?' Amara asked grimly.

'I do have a choice,' Iolanthe returned, and then closed her eyes against the realisation. She could tell Alekos that Niko was his son. Would he keep Petra Innovation for his own son? Could she gamble on some hidden compassion and softness that Alekos had yet to show her? And it *was* a gamble; she didn't know if she dared risk whatever repercussions such an admission would cause. Everything felt fraught.

'What do you mean, you have a choice?' Amara asked. 'If this man has the controlling shares...'

'I can talk to him.' Resolutely Iolanthe put down her cup of tea and squared her shoulders. 'I have to talk to him.'

After finishing her tea and talk with Amara, Iolanthe headed upstairs to the top floor of the town house that had been converted into a suite of rooms for Niko. She stopped in the doorway of his bedroom, watching him with a familiar ache in her heart. He was at his desk, his golden-brown gaze narrowed as he studied the code on the computer screen, completely absorbed in what he was doing, unaware of his surroundings or her presence.

'Niko.' Iolanthe spoke gently, knowing her son needed a little time to focus on a person after staring so long at a screen. 'What are you doing, *pethi mou*?'

Niko tensed at the sound of her voice and then slowly turned away from the screen, blinking his mother into focus. 'An app.'

'You're making another app?'

He nodded, his expression serious and a little wary. Social interaction had always been fraught for him. 'Which one is it this time?' Iolanthe asked lightly. She perched on the edge of the desk, making sure to stay well away from the computer Niko loved and obsessed over. Once she'd dared to touch the keyboard and a near meltdown had ensued. She knew better now.

Niko shrugged thin shoulders, his gaze sliding away from hers as it so often did. From the time he was a baby, Iolanthe had struggled to forge that connection that so many mothers took for granted. She loved her son, she had no doubt about that. She loved him with a fierce and aching fury, wanting to protect him because he was different, because there were so many things he didn't understand. But she didn't always feel that Niko loved her. Sometimes she wondered if her son knew how to love. She felt guilty and mean for the thought; Niko showed love in his own way. She *knew* that, had argued the point fiercely to Lukas and her father, and yet in the quiet grief of her own heart she wondered. She feared.

'Niko?' Iolanthe prompted gently. 'What's the app?'

He shrugged, looking away from her. 'Just a thing to keep track of your zombie power points.'

'Right.' As if she knew what that meant. In the last year Niko had started designing apps for some of the more popular online games, one of them apparently involving zombies. At Iolanthe's encouragement, he'd shown them to Lukas, shyly, but Lukas had dismissed them and him with one cursory glance. Iolanthe feared that Niko, in his silence and isolation, had absorbed his father's rejection, and it made him withdraw even more. She tried to support and encourage Niko as best she could, but she'd been out of her depth with his technical knowledge for years. 'So what are power points?' she asked. 'Are they good or bad?'

'Good. People buy them online for a lot of money.'

'Wow. And your app keeps track of them?'

Niko confirmed this with a little nod, his gaze already moving back to the computer screen.

'That sounds cool, Niko,' Iolanthe said, and dared to touch her son's hair with the tips of her fingertips.

He ducked away and Iolanthe withdrew her hand. 'Did you meet with the solicitor?' he asked after a few seconds, his gaze still on the screen.

'Yes.' She'd told him about her meeting last night before bed.

Niko turned to glance at her, his golden eyes, so much like Alekos's, narrowing. 'And what did he say? Is everything all right?'

'Everything's fine, Niko,' Iolanthe assured him. How could she tell him anything else? He might act as if he were much older in some ways, but her son was *nine*. She couldn't burden him with her financial troubles. Except they were his too, because Petra Innovation was meant to be his. Needed to be his. Taking that away from Niko would be like taking away his reason to live. Talking about Petra Innovation made his eyes light with excitement and brought him out of his untouchable silence to something close to a chatterbox. Niko *needed* Petra Innovation. He needed the hope of something better and bigger that he could be a part of.

Briefly Iolanthe closed her eyes as regret swamped through her. How had Lukas let this happen? How had *she*? Maybe she should have taken more of an interest in the company, insisted on knowing what was going on, and in doing so safeguarded her son's inheritance.

The prospect was, she knew, laughable. She didn't know the first thing about the business. And her father and Lukas would have never countenanced her interest anyway. They'd barely tolerated her presence, always reminding her of her shame.

'Mama?' The endearment sounded strange on her son's lips; he rarely used it. 'Are you sure everything is all right?'

'Yes.' Iolanthe took a deep breath and smiled at her son. She would not burden Niko with this. She would figure out a way to keep Petra Innovation for her son. She owed it to him to keep his dream alive; she owed it to herself. She'd given up so much already, all in payment for her crimes—the crime of giving her body to a cold and cruel man. 'Everything's fine, Niko.' She patted his hand, winning a shy, uncertain smile from him that felt like a triumph. Smiling back, she rose from her perch on his desk, leaving him to his app.

Somehow she had to find a way forward.

Alekos pushed his laptop away, disgusted with himself and his inability to concentrate since seeing Iolanthe yesterday. After leaving the offices of Petra Innovation, he'd wandered the streets of Athens' business district, too restless and on edge to return to his own office. Too beset by memories.

Memories of Iolanthe, her face, her voice, her body. Her throaty laugh, like strains of music he hadn't realised he still longed to hear. Her mouth, opening under his, a flower whose scent and nectar he realised he'd never forgotten. And the feel of him inside her, the way she'd accepted him into her body, and how in that moment he'd felt, powerful and vulnerable at the same time, as if he'd scaled a mountain and come home all at once.

How had he forgotten all that? Why had he remembered it now? Iolanthe had changed. *He* had changed. And he had no use for her any more, if he ever had.

Now he rose from his desk in the penthouse office of Demetriou Tech and gazed out at the city skyline. He could see the ancient Acropolis in the distance, and he recalled how he'd seen it that night with Iolanthe on the balcony, when he'd been desperate to kiss her. He just hadn't realised how much until his lips had touched hers.

Alekos swore under his breath and spun away from the window. He had to stop thinking this way. He had to stop remembering so damn much. And probably remembering it better than it was—it had been a single night of madness, a sexual encounter he'd been quick to dismiss as soon as it was over. No point in making more of it than there ever had been.

And yet he still felt restless. Where was the sense of satisfaction, of justice finally served? He'd been waiting for the day he was able to shut the doors on Petra Innovation for nearly fifteen years. When Callos had offered the shares on the open market six months ago, Alekos had known he finally had his chance.

Yet leaving Iolanthe in the CEO's office, he hadn't felt the savage surge of satisfaction he'd both craved and expected. He'd felt...empty. Cheated, even, although he couldn't say how or why.

'Kyria Iolanthe Callos to see you, sir.' The voice of his PA coming through the intercom had Alekos stiffening. Iolanthe had come here—why? To beg for Petra Innovation?

His mouth curved in a grim smile. Then he would let her beg.

Iolanthe stepped through the double doors into Alekos's office and forced both her step and voice to stay steady. It took a lot of effort. Just the sight of him standing there, one hand resting on his desk, his face so cold and closed and *beautiful*, made her heart flutter in her chest and every calm, confident thing she'd been planning to say empty from her head.

He looked forbidding but he also looked devastatingly attractive in his navy pinstriped, three-piece suit, his ebony hair cut close and emphasising his sharp cheekbones, those tawny eyes that his son had inherited. His mouth was a hard line but Iolanthe remembered when it had been soft and open on hers. She remembered the way his fingers had felt stroking her cheek...

'What are you doing here, Iolanthe?'

He didn't sound *quite* as unfriendly as he had that awful night when she'd come by, thinking to tell him she was pregnant. Recalling how harsh and unwelcoming he'd looked then thankfully forced away the memory of his kisses.

'I wanted to talk to you.' To her relief her voice came out strong. Mostly.

'I didn't realise we had anything to talk about.'

'Why do you want to liquidate Petra Innovation?' She hadn't meant to speak so plainly, so desperately. She'd meant to come from a stronger stance so they could have a civilised discussion among equals, and she could act as if she were in control. But why bother? They both knew she wasn't.

Alekos regarded her for a long, level moment, those

opaque golden eyes giving nothing away. 'Because it serves no purpose.'

'Then why did you buy it all? Why buy something just to sell it?'

'To make a profit.'

'Did you? After buying up all those shares?' Iolanthe's stomach cramped as the realisation hit her afresh. 'It really is just revenge,' she stated, and Alekos simply kept giving her that awful blank stare. 'It's always been about revenge for you.'

He cocked his head, his gaze sweeping over her, cold, closed, formidable. 'Then you know.'

'I know you've hated my father for having an idea you couldn't come up with,' Iolanthe fired back, too angry now to guard her words. 'For not being as fast or as clever as he was. It's not just revenge, it's—it's nothing more than sour grapes!'

Alekos's expression didn't change and yet he seemed even more still, more dangerous, like a predator about to spring and devour. 'What do you mean by that?' he asked in an ominously low voice.

Iolanthe quelled underneath that voice and gaze but she still held her ground. 'He told me all about the history between you two, after...' She trailed away, a treacherous flush sweeping over her entire body as she remembered that *after.* After she'd given herself to Alekos, body and soul. After she'd stupidly thought they had some kind of connection, some kind of future.

'He told you about our history?' Alekos clarified. 'And he said I wasn't as—what was it?—as fast or as clever as he was?'

'Yes...'

He strolled to the window, his hands clasped behind his back, and gazed out at the azure sky. 'He came up with an idea that I couldn't.'

Iolanthe eyed him uncertainly. He'd spoken the words

like a statement, but it felt more like a question. Something was still unsaid, unresolved. 'Something like that. He didn't give me the details. He just said there was a software system he'd designed more quickly than you had.'

'Is that right?' He sounded so diffident, as if this were a matter of casual interest, yet she could feel the tension and even the anger reverberating through the room. The air felt electric with it.

'So you think my taking over Petra Innovation is payback for your father being better than me?' Alekos stated. 'For coming up with an idea I couldn't?' Iolanthe didn't answer and Alekos turned around, his mouth twisting. 'What a sad, petty little man you must think I am.'

Sad, petty, little. None of those words described Alekos Demetriou. And yet he'd been so hard and hostile towards her in every interaction after their first. What was she supposed to believe? 'Are you saying I shouldn't believe him?' she challenged. 'That he was lying to me? He was my father—'

'Whereas I was only the man you slept with. The man you gave your virginity to.' His mouth curved cynically and Iolanthe battled a rising wave of fury.

'And you made it very clear what you thought of that ill-fated gift,' she snapped. 'Trust me, I don't regret anything more.'

'I can say the same.'

'Well, then.' She was breathing heavily, her chest rising and falling in agitated breaths as she glared at him. This was not the way she'd wanted to conduct this meeting.

'Well, then,' Alekos repeated mockingly. He inclined his head, that cynical smile still touching his lips. 'It seems we have nothing more to say to one another.'

'But we do.' Iolanthe glared at him in frustration. 'You can't do this, Alekos—'

'So you've said before, but you'll find that I can.'

'Why?' She heard the ragged note of tears in her voice

and swallowed it down. She had no time for tears, and she was quite sure Alekos didn't either. Not hers, anyway. 'Why destroy my father's company, my son's livelihood, for something that happened years and years ago? So he designed something you were trying to. He beat you. Can't you just let it go?'

'Yes, he *beat* me,' Alekos returned, a savage note entering his voice. 'He did that.'

Iolanthe eyed him uncertainly. 'Why are you so angry still?'

His face cleared of emotion, his voice toneless when he spoke. 'In any case, it's hardly as if you'll be out on the street. I estimate that your forty per cent, when liquidated, will bring in enough profit to leave you far from destitute.'

'I don't want *money*,' Iolanthe cried. 'I want my father's company for my son. It's his birthright, Alekos—'

'Then perhaps your husband should have taken better care of it.'

He was so implacable, so terribly cold. 'Damn you,' Iolanthe choked, and she pressed her fist to her lips as she struggled for control. She had to tell Alekos about Niko. Even now, especially now, she shrank from the idea, from the prospect of Alekos's disbelief or, far worse, his rejection of his son.

Or, she acknowledged sickly, an even more terrifying possibility…that Alekos would want some say in his son's life. In *her* life.

She didn't know which option scared her the most. And so she stayed silent, her back to Alekos, her fist still pressed to her mouth as she drew several deep breaths.

'I really don't see why you care so much,' Alekos said and she stiffened. 'Your son is what? Seven? Eight?'

'Nine,' Iolanthe whispered.

'A child,' Alekos stated. 'He will be well provided for with the money that remains. You don't need to worry about that. Or is it just that you don't want me to have it?'

Iolanthe turned around slowly. 'I don't want you to *destroy* it,' she clarified. 'Can't you understand that?'

Alekos stared at her, unmoved. 'No, I can't. It isn't as if it was your business. All it did was fund your lifestyle.'

Iolanthe drew back, stung by the scornful words. 'My lifestyle?' she repeated. 'And you know so much about that?'

He shrugged. 'A town house in the Plaka, a private island...'

Iolanthe let out a hollow laugh. 'You are listing my husband's assets, not my lifestyle.'

Alekos folded his arms. 'All I'm saying is you won't be inconvenienced. Your lifestyle won't change, or at least not too much.'

She stared at him in disbelief. 'My husband is dead, his company is about to be destroyed, and you think my *lifestyle* won't change? You are either the most unintelligent or the most insensitive man I've ever met. Maybe both.'

'I'm sorry.' A muscle flickered in his jaw before he set it. 'I was not referring to the death of your husband. Just the company.'

'Oh, okay. That's fine, then.' Iolanthe let out another laugh, this one ragged. Alekos had no idea about her life, how quiet and simple it had been. Clearly he thought she was some pampered princess, a spoilt heiress enjoying society life.

How could she tell Alekos about Niko? Yet how could she not? Petra Innovation was *everything* to Niko. He lived for the day he'd be able to take the helm. But what if telling Alekos the truth didn't change his mind?

And what if it did?

'It seems there is nothing more to say,' Alekos said flatly.

Iolanthe took a deep breath. 'Actually, Alekos, there is.' Another breath to fill her lungs; she felt as if she were jumping off a cliff, stepping out into thin air. How long would she freefall for? And how hard would her landing be? 'Niko isn't Lukas Callos's son, Alekos. He's yours.'

CHAPTER SIX

ALEKOS HEARD THE words as if from a great distance. They echoed in his head as he stared at her in nonplussed confusion. Finally he managed, 'You must really be desperate.'

She flinched, her eyes flashing, courage and fear together. 'You don't believe me.'

'Why should I?'

'Why would I lie? It's easy enough to prove.'

Her calm certainty unnerved him as much as her initial statement had left him reeling. 'You mean a paternity test.'

Silver eyes flashed again, and she pressed her lips together. 'That's exactly what I mean.'

For a few seconds Alekos was left completely speechless. 'Why would you keep such a thing from me?' he finally asked, his voice low and vibrating with suppressed emotion—far too much emotion to process. He didn't know what to feel. Anger at Iolanthe for keeping something this huge from him? Wonder that he had a *child*? Incredulity was easier.

'I tried to tell you back then,' Iolanthe answered. Her voice shook but she kept his gaze. 'When I came to your flat.'

'You *tried*? You didn't say anything of the sort!' He took a deep breath, recalling that brief, tense interview. He'd been so angry, still smarting from her father's shameful treatment of him, suspecting her part in the deception. And she... She'd been afraid. He remembered how she'd trembled, how her eyes had looked huge in her pale face. He'd told her to leave and she had, fleeing from the room as if he were chasing her out with a stick. 'I asked you,' he said, recalling that too. 'I specifically asked you if you were carrying my child.'

'And then you said if I wasn't, I should leave immediately,' Iolanthe fired back. 'Hardly the friendliest of exchanges.'

'We've never been friends,' Alekos returned coolly. 'But I expected an honest answer to my question.'

'Why should I have answered you at all?' Iolanthe demanded. 'You clearly despised me.' She took a deep breath, pressing a pale hand to her forehead. 'But I don't want to talk about that now. I want to know if you'll keep Petra Innovation for Niko, since he's your son.'

'You have no compunction in showing your hand,' Alekos observed. 'The only reason you're telling me he's mine is because of the company. Because of what you want from me.'

'Yes.' She was completely unabashed. 'I want Niko to have his birthright.'

Alekos's lip curled. 'How is it even his birthright, if he is not biologically related to Lukas Callos?'

'I often wonder,' Iolanthe returned, her lips pinched and bloodless, 'how you charmed me that night. Because you certainly haven't done so since.'

'I wonder that I charmed you at all,' Alekos snapped. 'Or did *you* set out to be charmed, even seduced?'

Iolanthe shook her head slowly, confusion visible in her silvery eyes. 'Why would I do that?'

'I have no idea. Perhaps you wanted to frame me, or humiliate your father—'

'What—?'

'I know he kept you locked away, on leading strings. Was sleeping with me your childish way of getting back at him?' He shrugged, not caring about her answer. Not wanting to care. 'In any case I have learned not to trust anyone in your forsaken family.' He turned away abruptly, not wanting to say more. He wasn't going to whinge to

Iolanthe about how her father had welcomed him into the Petra Innovation fold before stealing his idea fourteen years ago, leaving him desolate in so many ways. Grieving the loss of his livelihood, the loss of the friendship of a man he'd trusted. Most likely she wouldn't believe him anyway, and, in any case, he'd had his revenge already. It just didn't feel as sweet as he'd anticipated.

'Will you require a paternity test?' Iolanthe asked after a moment. She sounded tired, as if the fight had left her. Alekos turned around, noticing the way her slender shoulders sagged. She looked as if a breath would blow her over. Yet even as weary as she obviously was, she was still lovely. She wore a navy sheath dress that emphasised her willowy figure. She'd pulled her hair back with a clip, and a few inky tendrils curled about her heart-shaped face.

'Of course I will,' Alekos returned. Again he was struck by how unfazed she was by the prospect. She seemed unnervingly certain…and there could only be one reason why.

'And when you receive the result?' Iolanthe asked. 'Will you then keep from liquidating Petra Innovation?'

His mind scrambled to make sense of how quickly things had progressed. A son. He could not imagine it, could not *conceive—*

And yet Iolanthe *had* conceived—and had never told him. It was a deception that he could barely grasp the enormity of, worse than anything she might have done before.

'I will not make any decisions until your son's paternity is known for certain.'

'Fine. It should only take a few days. But in the meantime, promise me you won't do anything to dispose of Petra Innovation.'

Alekos opened his mouth to retort that he would make no promises whatsoever, but then he stopped. If Niko was his son, he needed to completely rethink his plans. The realisation of how much could change left him scrambling for both words and thoughts. 'Fine,' he finally bit out.

Iolanthe nodded her acceptance. 'Do you wish to make the arrangements for the test, or shall I?'

'I'll do it.'

'Thank you.' Iolanthe turned to go, and Alekos had the bizarre impulse to call out to her, make her stay. To say... what? He had no idea. There was nothing between them now...except perhaps, amazingly, a child.

'I'm sorry, Iolanthe.'

Iolanthe closed her eyes, pressing her fingers to the lids as she battled a wave of fatigue. She felt too tired for shock or even sorrow; the bad news just seemed to keep on coming. 'It's all right, Antonis,' she said. Some time over the last week, as the true and terrible state of Lukas's affairs had come to light, she and her solicitor had progressed to first names. 'It's not your fault.'

'He never told me...'

'It's all right.'

A few more pointless pleasantries and she hung up the phone, her mind spinning. Lukas had not only led the company into financial difficulty, but he'd done the same with his personal assets as well. Antonis had been looking into his client's financial situation all week, and none of the news was good.

The savings account that had held her inheritance from her father was empty, their luxurious town house remortgaged, the private island Alekos had mocked given back to the bank. The only thing she had left was her forty per cent of Petra Innovation. But she still didn't want to sell it.

Letting out a shuddering breath, she rose from her chair in the small morning room that she'd taken as a private parlour and crossed to the window that was open to the early summer's night. The sultry air caressed her bare arms and she leaned her forehead against the shutter, wondering how Lukas could have behaved so foolishly. Left her with so little.

And what about Alekos? She hadn't heard from him in four days, after he'd arranged a doctor to come and collect a swab from Niko's cheek for the paternity test. Niko had been nonplussed, and Iolanthe had stammered some explanation about checking for diseases, treating it like some kind of vaccination. Thankfully Niko had just shrugged and gone back to his computer. But what about Alekos? He had to know by now that Niko was his son. Why hadn't he contacted her?

Feeling cold despite the warm breeze, Iolanthe turned from the window. Perhaps she shouldn't have told Alekos about Niko; she felt as if she'd opened up a Pandora's Box of possibilities that she would never be able to control. She wished she knew what he intended, whether he'd reject Niko or be more involved in his life. Which possibility alarmed her more?

A light knock sounded on the door. 'Iolanthe?'

'Come in, Amara.'

The housekeeper opened the door, frowning at Iolanthe. 'There is a man here to see you,' Amara said. 'He said his name is Alekos Demetriou. I've put him in the drawing room, but I can send him away...'

Iolanthe's heart lurched, her hands going clammy. So Alekos had come after all...but for what purpose? 'No, it's all right. I'll see him.'

Amara's mouth tightened and she planted her hands on her ample hips. 'This is the man who will destroy Kyrie Petrakis's company?'

'Liquidate it, yes. But I'm hoping I might have changed his mind.'

Amara looked doubtful. 'Shall I serve tea?'

'No, I don't think so.' She had no idea what Alekos intended to say, and she didn't want to make him welcome until she did. 'Thank you, Amara.'

The housekeeper withdrew and Iolanthe glanced in the mirror, ran a hand over her hair. She wasn't in one of her few designer outfits to bolster her confidence; she'd been at home all day and wore jeans and a pale pink scalloped-edged T-shirt, with no make-up or jewellery. She wished she were dressed more professionally. She needed the armour.

She went downstairs, trying to quell the nerves that jangled at seeing Alekos again. Taking a deep breath, she opened the door, and then stopped short at the sight of him.

Gone was the high-powered and hard-polished CEO in his three-thousand-euro suit. Instead Alekos, like her, wore jeans and a T-shirt, his hair mussed as if he'd raked a hand through it, his face haggard.

Carefully Iolanthe shut the door behind her. 'I take it you received the results of the paternity test.'

'Yes.' Alekos scrubbed his hands through his hair, making it stand up on end even more. 'Why didn't you tell me, Iolanthe?' he demanded in a raw voice. 'Back then?'

Iolanthe blinked, startled by this new Alekos, one she'd never seen before. 'I told you why not.'

'But a child. A *son*.' His voice, already ragged, broke on the word. 'How could you keep such a thing from me?'

Guilt sliced through her at the sound of emotion in his voice. Over the years she hadn't let herself think about just how much she'd been depriving Alekos of by not telling him about his son. She hadn't let herself think of Alekos at all. 'I was afraid,' she said. 'And very young—'

'Neither is an excuse.' Alekos cut across her, his voice turning hard and unforgiving. 'You knew this would change everything. I told you it would, on that very night. I told you I wanted to know—'

'And then you tried to drive me away. You weren't interested in me or anything I had to say. Be fair, Alekos.'

'You want to talk about *fair*?' he demanded, his voice an angry throb.

Iolanthe took a deep breath. 'No, I want to talk about what's going to happen now.' Of course he couldn't understand her perspective. He'd never been interested in her point of view, in her as a person. He'd taken her virginity and then kicked her to the door. And now he had the gall to blame her for everything. 'Why are you here, Alekos?'

'I want to meet my son.'

The starkly stated desire had Iolanthe stilling in shock. Yet what had she expected? That Alekos would keep Petra Innovation for Niko but walk away from the boy? She'd known what she was risking by telling Alekos the truth. She just hadn't let herself face it.

'You won't deny me that,' Alekos added, an ominous note entering his voice.

Iolanthe crossed the room to sink onto one of the velvet sofas. She felt as if her legs couldn't hold her weight any longer. 'No, I won't deny you that,' she said after a moment, when she trusted her voice to sound steady. 'I knew in telling you, you'd want access to Niko.'

'Access?' Aleko repeated, and Iolanthe heard derision. 'You think I want *access*?'

Iolanthe gazed at him uncertainly; his hair was still sticking up and his mouth was twisted with contempt but even so he looked shockingly handsome. The plain grey T-shirt clung to the sculpted muscles of his chest and the faded jeans moulded to his powerful legs. He radiated angry authority, barely leashed power. She admired his form even as she quaked inwardly. He *scared* her.

'I thought that was what you were saying...'

'If you think,' Alekos said, taking a step towards her, 'that I'm going to settle for some arrangement of occasional supervised visits with my son, you are more naïve than you were ten years ago.'

'We can discuss the arrangements, of course,' Iolanthe said after a pause. Alekos was glaring at her, his fists clenched, everything about him angry and accusing, and she had the terrible suspicion that she'd made things worse by telling him the truth of his son. Much worse. 'Antonis, my solicitor—'

'Don't bring your damned solicitor into this, Iolanthe.'

She blinked, struck by his savage tone. 'Naturally we'll have to negotiate—'

'No.' The word was flat, unyielding, without so much as a whisper of compromise.

Iolanthe drew herself up. She wasn't twenty years old and cringingly naïve any more. 'This isn't another corporate takeover, Alekos. You can't bully me. We'll agree to terms—'

'You forfeited the right to agree to terms when you hid the truth from me for ten years,' he cut across her, his words like a whip, scourging her and making her flinch. 'I don't negotiate, Iolanthe. Not in business and definitely not about this.'

She stared at him, her stomach churning so hard she felt she might be sick. She pressed her hand to her middle and took a few needed deep breaths. 'You have to admit to some compromise, Alekos,' she said as evenly as she could. 'It doesn't do Niko any good for us to be fighting over every little thing.'

'We won't fight.'

She eyed him in disbelief. 'All we've done since we laid eyes on each other again is fight.' She shook her head, fatigue warring with frustration. 'I don't even know why you seem to despise me so much.'

Alekos didn't answer and Iolanthe glanced at him, surprised to see an emotion other than anger etched on his face. He almost looked...sorry.

'I don't despise you,' he said gruffly.

'But we've never been friends.' Wearily Iolanthe parroted back his earlier words. 'Still, for Niko's sake, we need to make this as friendly as possible. You must see that, Alekos, no matter what you say about not negotiating.'

'We'll keep it friendly,' Alekos promised, and for some reason his words caused alarm to ripple through her.

'Thank you,' she said, even though she felt as if she was waiting for the next blow.

'We'll keep it very friendly,' Alekos continued. 'Because I'm not going to be sidelined out of my son's life.'

'I never said—'

'What were you thinking?' Alekos demanded. 'A weekend here, an evening there?'

Iolanthe blinked at him. 'I wasn't really thinking at all,' she admitted. 'Not that practically. I just wanted to keep Petra Innovation for my son.'

He let out a harsh laugh. 'So at least I know you weren't thinking about *me*.'

'I'm sure that's a relief,' Iolanthe returned. 'You made it clear you didn't want my affection—'

'Ten years ago,' he finished, his tone one of curt dismissal. 'You do realise that Niko is the heir not just to Petra Innovation, but Demetriou Tech?' Alekos met her gaze, his eyes like burning embers, singeing her.

Shocked realisation sliced through her. 'You would make him your heir…?'

'I don't have another.'

'But you might marry,' Iolanthe protested. 'You might have other children—'

'I will marry,' Alekos affirmed. 'And I will have other children. But Niko is my firstborn son, and he will be my heir.'

The coolly stated fact that he would marry put both Iolanthe's head and heart in a spin, which was ridiculous, of course. Alekos was thirty-six years old. Of course he would marry at some point, and probably soon. Maybe he even had a woman already, waiting in the wings, ready and eager to become Kyria Demetriou. It had nothing to do with her.

'You sound very sure,' she said after a moment. 'You haven't even met Niko.'

'I know he's my son.'

Iolanthe tried to gather her scattered thoughts. 'But what about this potential bride of yours? She might want the children you have together to—'

'My potential bride,' Alekos cut across her, his voice like a blade, 'will want Niko as my heir.'

Iolanthe stared at him, flummoxed. 'How—?'

'Because,' he continued implacably, 'my prospective bride, my only bride, is you.'

CHAPTER SEVEN

For a few stunned seconds Iolanthe thought Alekos was joking. He had to be joking—and yet looking at the steel that had entered both his jaw and his eyes, his arms folded across his chest, his gaze clashing with hers... There was nothing funny about this situation. This was no joke.

Still she gasped out, 'You can't be serious.'

'I assure you I am.'

'*Marriage?* Alekos, you don't even like me.'

'We will put our differences aside for the sake of our son.'

'By your decree?' Iolanthe rejoined. 'I don't have any say in this?'

'I assume you want what is best for Niko.'

'Emotional blackmail,' Iolanthe stated flatly. Just as her father and Lukas had both done, in their different ways, forcing her into a marriage she hadn't wanted. The thought of another loveless union, and this time to Alekos, made her feel faint and sick. 'You know I want what's best for him,' she managed shakily. 'Of course I do. But marriage to you is not necessarily it.'

'I think it is.'

Her temper began to flare. 'Then maybe we'll have to disagree.'

Her gaze clashed and tangled with his, and as Iolanthe refused to look away from his burning gold gaze she felt a sudden heat slice through her, reminding her of how this man had touched her. Tasted and moved inside her. And she knew in that moment that she was still attracted to him, that she still felt the magnetic pull of desire she'd felt ten years ago, only now it was even more inconvenient. More unwelcome.

Drawing a hand across her forehead, she rose from the sofa and walked away from him, desperate to compose her thoughts.

Marriage. 'I've only just buried my first husband, you know.'

'We will observe propriety. A three-month engagement should suffice.'

'Three months?' She let out a hollow laugh. 'Considering I was married to Lukas for ten years, that's not very long.'

'I won't wait any longer.'

'Of course not.' She shook her head, bemused and overwhelmed and too tired to think through any of it now. Alekos wouldn't let the matter rest, though. She knew enough about him to understand that. 'You can't just spring this on me, Alekos, and expect me to fall in with your plans immediately.' She'd been falling in with other people's plans her whole life. She supposed she shouldn't have been surprised that nothing had changed. *She* hadn't changed, because already she was considering Alekos's proposal, if she could even use that word. Command seemed more appropriate. Already guilt was burrowing its way into her soul, whispering that she should do anything for her son. Of course she should. Any decent mother would.

'I don't see what there is to think about,' Alekos stated. 'The solution seems perfectly obvious to me.'

She whirled around, pushed past endurance by his utter inflexibility. 'You might think so, but that doesn't mean I do. Perhaps I'm not willing to agree to marriage to a stranger ten seconds after I've received the most unromantic proposal on the planet!'

Alekos met her wild gaze with a level one of his own. 'It wasn't meant to be romantic.'

Iolanthe laughed, the sound utterly without humour. 'I do realise that, thank you.'

He eyed her with consideration, his head cocked to one side. 'Is that what you want? Romance? Love?'

She let out her breath in a low rush. Love wasn't something she'd let herself think about in a long, long time. 'No, not really.' Her brief brush with love—sexual love, anyway—had been a disaster. And ten years of coldness and solitude had made her too numb ever to hope for more. *And certainly not with Alekos.*

'Did you love Callos?' He spoke diffidently, as if it didn't really matter. Iolanthe looked away, not wanting to reveal the pointless sorrow of her marriage. 'Well?' he prompted, and she knew he wouldn't leave it.

'No.' In the beginning she'd tried to get along with him, but it had taken only days to realise Lukas had no interest in her whatsoever. He'd married her to secure his future with her father's company, that was all.

'Did he know he wasn't Niko's father?'

'Yes. I never pretended about that. He married me knowing I carried another man's child.' For that alone she'd tried to respect Lukas, but he'd done precious little in their ten years to keep her respect—or earn her affection.

'So you married him to provide a father for Niko.' The words sounded bitter, an accusation.

'Yes, and because my father wished it.' Had commanded it. 'I didn't have a lot of options, Alekos, after what I'd done.'

'You mean what we'd done.'

She looked at him, startled to hear a note of recrimination in his voice. Was he acknowledging guilt—or just stating a fact? 'Yes,' she said after a pause. 'What we'd done.'

Alekos nodded slowly, saying nothing. Iolanthe braced herself for another round of fighting, another set of impossible demands. 'Did you ever do anything with your art?'

he asked and she blinked, completely taken aback by this sudden turn in the conversation.

'My art...'

'You told me, that night, that art was your favourite subject. And that you wanted to do something important.'

She let out an uncertain laugh. 'I'm surprised you remembered what I said back then. I must have sounded very silly and young.'

'You sounded hopeful.' Alekos's voice was flat, almost bleak, his expression as inscrutable as ever. Iolanthe had no idea what to make of his remarks.

'I suppose I was. I've learned better since then.' As soon as she said the words she wished she hadn't. She wasn't bitter. At least, she tried not to be.

Alekos gazed at her for a long moment, and Iolanthe braced herself for more questions about her marriage. 'May I see him?' he asked quietly.

'Niko—?'

'Yes.'

This was not his usual intractable demand, but instead a quiet and sincere plea, and it cut Iolanthe to the heart. 'He's sleeping now...'

'Let me just see him,' Alekos insisted, his voice low and urgent. 'I won't wake him up. We can discuss how best to introduce me to him later.' He gazed at her, and this time his burning stare held no anger, just desperation.

Iolanthe swallowed hard and then nodded. She'd denied Alekos so much already. 'Yes, you can see him. I'll show you the way.'

Silently she opened the doors to the drawing room and headed upstairs, Alekos following behind her. Amara had already gone to bed, and the lights had all been turned off save for one small table lamp in the hall that cast a warm glow and lent an intimate air to the moment.

Iolanthe was very conscious of Alekos walking behind her; she breathed in the scent of his aftershave and felt both the heat and tension from his body. Remembered all sorts of things—how surprisingly sleek and soft his skin had been, how his arms around her had felt both gentle and powerful; he was a man who could leash his strength. How for an evening she'd felt treasured and important, just as she'd told him she wanted to be. He'd made her feel that way.

And then afterwards he made you feel like something stuck to his shoe.

She couldn't forget that. She needed to remember it, if she was going to navigate this fraught relationship with any hope of success. Iolanthe turned down the hallway to Niko's set of rooms. She paused, her hand on the doorknob of his bedroom. 'I don't want you to disturb him.'

'I won't wake him up,' Alekos promised. 'I just want to see him.'

'I know…' Still Iolanthe hesitated. She felt as if opening this door would be the first step down a long and uncertain road. But perhaps she'd taken that step when she'd told Alekos about Niko. Perhaps now there was no other road to travel, no other step to take. With a single nod of acceptance, Iolanthe pushed open the door.

The room was lit only by the moonlight spilling through the window, barely illuminating the room with its military-level of neatness. No spilled Lego, no half-finished games or projects. Niko hated mess, craved order.

Iolanthe watched as Alekos stepped into the room, his gaze searching out the slight form on the single bed. Niko lay on his side, legs tucked up, one hand resting by his cheek. He looked vulnerable and innocent and so very young.

Alekos moved closer to his son, and the moonlight washed over the hard lines and angles of his face; he almost looked as if he were in pain, gripped as he was by emotion.

He reached a hand out to Niko's face and Iolanthe held

her breath. If Niko woke up… Alekos brushed his son's cheek with the tips of his fingers and Niko stirred, letting out a breathy sigh before rolling over. Alekos stepped back into the shadows, his gaze sweeping over the room before he turned to Iolanthe and nodded.

She led the way out, pausing by the door with one hand on the knob to shut it after Alekos had gone. He moved past her, his shoulder brushing her breast, and the flash of desire Iolanthe felt made her draw her breath in sharply.

Alekos turned, and his mouth was close enough to hers that all she'd have to do to kiss him was tilt her head. She felt the strength of his stare, the force of his feeling. It felt like a laser, piercing her to the core, pinning her in place. How was it that after a decade apart she could still feel this way? And he did too, judging by the heat in his eyes, the way he angled himself towards her.

No matter that it had been ten years and they didn't even like each other. The attraction, the overwhelming force of it, was still there.

With effort Iolanthe looked away from Alekos as she pulled the door closed. The soft click of it shutting brought them both out of the moment, and Alekos turned towards the stairs.

Iolanthe let out the breath she'd been holding and willed her heart to slow. That had been close.

She followed Alekos downstairs, expecting him to head for the front door but he returned to the drawing room instead. Iolanthe followed him, steeling herself for another altercation.

'I want to meet Niko tomorrow.'

'I need to prepare him—'

'You don't need to tell him I'm his father yet,' Alekos cut across her. 'But I want to meet him. Talk to him.'

Slowly Iolanthe moved into the room. Emotional and physical fatigue crashed over her and she sank into a chair, her head in her hands.

'Iolanthe…?' Concern mingled with impatience sharpened Alekos's voice.

'I'm *tired*, Alekos. It's eleven o'clock at night and I've been dealing with so much…'

'What have you been dealing with?'

She thought of Antonis's earlier phone call and the hard reality of her financial situation. If Alekos found out how desperate she was, he might press her to marry him even more. He'd know she was running out of choices, just as her father once had. She couldn't bear to be backed into another corner.

'Just…business things,' she said, to put him off. 'Lukas's estate, and Niko losing the man he thought was his father. It's a lot to process.'

'You never told him the truth?'

'No, of course not. He's only nine, after all, and Lukas acted as a father to him.' Barely.

Alekos's mouth tightened. 'Do you know what it does to me, to know that another man, a man I despise, was able to be the father to my son when I was denied?' He pinched the bridge of his nose as he drew in a shuddering breath. 'I don't know if I can ever forgive that, Iolanthe.'

'Then we certainly shouldn't get married,' Iolanthe retorted. The last thing she wanted was to enter another relationship based on guilt and fear. 'Why do you despise Lukas? I didn't think you even knew him.'

'I didn't,' Alekos answered flatly. 'But I knew what he did.'

Unease churned in her stomach and crept cold fingers up her spine. 'What are you talking about, Alekos?'

Alekos stared at her for a long moment, his eyes opaque, his jaw set. 'Now is not the time for that particular discussion. I'll return here tomorrow to meet Niko. What time is he home from school?'

'He doesn't go to school.'

Straight, dark brows snapped together. 'He doesn't go
to school? Why not?'

'School has been...difficult for him.'

'Difficult?' Alekos's voice came out in a growl. 'What
are you saying? Has he had problems? Was he bullied?'

'No, no, nothing like that.' Iolanthe pressed her fingers
to her temples. She could feel the beginnings of a head-
ache. How could she explain Niko to Alekos? 'Niko didn't
perform well in school,' she began slowly. 'He had trouble
making friends, and sitting still and paying attention has
been hard for him.'

Alekos's mouth flattened. 'So he is badly behaved.'

'No,' Iolanthe fired back. 'That's not it at all. Some of
his teachers made that assumption, but the truth is much
more complicated than that.'

'Then tell me the truth.'

'It's hard to explain. Niko is just...different.' Doctors
had offered various diagnoses, but none had seemed to
fit. She stared at him unhappily. 'You'll understand when
you meet him tomorrow.'

Alekos looked as if he wanted to press the matter, but
then, to Iolanthe's relief, he merely gave a terse nod. 'I'll
come in the morning, then, around ten.'

'He's tutored until noon,' Iolanthe said and held up a
pacifying hand. 'But I'll take him out of his lessons. I
was just telling you so you know that he *is* learning. He's
doing well in his own environment.' And it had taken a
long time and a lot of effort, not to mention tears, heart-
ache, and worry, for her to be able to say that.

'We'll talk more tomorrow,' Alekos said, and to
Iolanthe it felt like a threat. What if Alekos rejected Niko
after meeting him? Her son was fiercely intelligent and
creative, but he could also be uncommunicative, awkward,
and high-maintenance. Lukas certainly hadn't had the
patience to deal with him—what if Alekos didn't either?
What if this all blew up in her face, and worse, in Niko's

face? She couldn't stand the thought of her son experiencing another rejection.

'Tomorrow,' Alekos said firmly, and Iolanthe nodded. She watched him leave the room, heard the click of the front door shutting. She felt a curious mixture of relief and disappointment; she was grateful for the reprieve but with Alekos gone she felt as if something vital had left the room. Left her life.

It was so dangerous, to think like that. To want like that. She remembered that moment upstairs, when for a few taut seconds she'd thought he might kiss her. She'd wanted him to kiss her.

And if they did marry...would he kiss her then? Would it be a marriage in the true sense of the word? Iolanthe couldn't believe she was even asking herself those questions. She couldn't marry Alekos. He'd made her feel like the most desirable woman on earth...and the least. She couldn't live with that kind of see-sawing emotion, and she certainly couldn't expose Niko to it.

But she had a sinking, certain feeling that Alekos would never let it go. Never let her or Niko go. She'd willingly walked into one gilded cage already. Perhaps it was no more than her duty to step into another.

CHAPTER EIGHT

ANTICIPATION AND ANXIETY warred within Alekos as he approached the front door of Iolanthe's town house the next morning to meet Niko. His *son.*

Seeing the boy last night had felt like a fist reaching right into his heart and squeezing hard. Niko's floppy dark hair had reminded him of his own as a child. He'd glimpsed a book on computer programming thrown by the bed and he'd remembered devouring similar manuals as a young boy. Niko was his more than just biologically. Already Alekos felt a connection to his child, one he'd never expected.

His own family had been fractured at a young age, his siblings split up after his father's death and farmed out to relatives, his mother working hard as a cleaner to keep body and soul together, and not much else. Family had never meant anything to him except inevitable disappointment, inherent rejection.

But this time it could be different. He certainly wouldn't abandon Niko the way his parents had, in different ways, abandoned him and his siblings. Resolutely Alekos knocked on the door.

The housekeeper he'd met briefly last night answered it, her wrinkled face set into lines of obvious disapproval. She gave him a short nod. 'Kyrie Demetriou.'

'I am here to see Iolanthe and Niko.'

The woman pressed her lips together. 'What business do you have with my mistress?' she burst out and Alekos drew back, surprised and affronted by the temerity of the question.

'I don't believe that's any of your concern.'

'It is my concern because she is my mistress and she has been through enough these last ten years,' the housekeeper declared. 'You seem like you will only cause her yet more grief.'

'I have no intention of doing anything of the sort,' Alekos answered, although he was surprised and a little shaken by the housekeeper's words. He realised how little he knew about Iolanthe's marriage. She'd said she hadn't loved Lukas, but had Lukas loved her? Or had it merely been a marriage of cold expediency—the boss's daughter in exchange for accepting her bastard child? Alekos didn't like to think of her marriage at all. Incredible that after a single night and ten years, he could feel so much as a twinge of jealousy.

Iolanthe met him in the drawing room where he'd seen her last night. Now, instead of looking casual and touchable in jeans and a lacy top, she wore a pair of tailored trousers and a high-necked blouse, clothes she clearly considered a defence against him. She'd drawn her hair back in a clip and although her lips were bright with lipstick her face looked pale. She was nervous, but then so was he. He was going to meet his son.

'I've told Niko you're a friend,' she said without preamble. 'For now. And that you're interested in computers. He loves them.'

'All right.'

Iolanthe clasped her hands together and met his gaze, her eyes bright with anxiety. 'I told you he's a bit different...'

'I know.' Alekos held up a hand. 'Let me meet him, Iolanthe, and see and judge for myself.'

She nodded as she released a low breath. 'Okay,' she said, and bit her lip, still clearly nervous.

Alekos had the bizarre urge to comfort her, even hold her. He was amazed at how natural it would feel, to pull her into his arms and stroke her hair. To tell her it was going to be okay, that he would take care of her.

He shook his head to clear it of that unsettling impulse. He wanted to marry Iolanthe for Niko's sake, but he didn't want to care about her. He knew where indulging in that kind of emotion led. His only interest was in his son.

'Where is he?'

'Upstairs, on the computer. It's probably best if we go up there.'

'Very well.'

Once again they climbed the staircase, this time with bright sunlight pouring through the window. Alekos took the opportunity to examine what he saw of Iolanthe's house, her life, but he couldn't tell much from the tasteful prints on the walls or the antique furniture. It looked bland to him, the home of someone rich and important, nothing else.

'Niko...?' Iolanthe called as she knocked on the door of the room next to his bedroom. 'Remember I told you Alekos was coming to meet you?' Shooting a quick, anxious smile at Alekos, she pushed open the door and entered the room.

Alekos followed, his gaze arrowing in on the little boy who sat in front of a computer monitor, his expression closed and wary.

'Hey.' Iolanthe smiled and stepped aside so Alekos could come more fully into the room. 'This is Alekos. A friend.'

Niko eyed Alekos silently. His eyes, Alekos saw with a jolt, were golden-brown, a similar colour to his own. He was slightly built, but then Alekos had been at that age as well. One hand rested possessively on the keyboard.

'Did you know my father?' he asked Alekos.

'I knew of him, but we'd never really met.' It took effort to keep his voice mild and friendly. The last thing he wanted to do was talk about Lukas.

'You work with computers?'

'Yes.' Niko's gaze flitted towards him and then away again, as if he was uncomfortable meeting Alekos's eye. Alekos tried not to feel the sting of rejection. He was too emotional for this meeting, too raw. 'Your mother told me you like computers?'

'Yes.' Niko had already turned back to the screen, clicking the mouse, having summarily dismissed Alekos.

'Niko…' Iolanthe began. 'Alekos is here to talk to you…'

'I don't want to talk to him.'

Alekos drew his breath in sharply at such rudeness. Iolanthe, he saw, looked pained but not surprised. So his son *was* badly behaved.

'He came all this way…'

'I don't want to.' A new, sharper note had entered Niko's voice and his hand clenched on the mouse. From across the room Alekos could see the tension in the little boy's body; he was practically vibrating with it.

'All right, Niko, all right,' Iolanthe soothed. She threw Alekos an apologetic and faintly panicked glance. He felt as if he was missing part of the conversation; something was happening that he didn't understand.

'We can talk later,' he offered, and Niko didn't reply. He had started to rock a little back and forth, one skinny arm wrapped around his middle. Iolanthe stepped towards her son.

'It's okay, Niko. You don't have to talk to anyone now.' She put her hand on his shoulder and Niko flinched away.

'Don't.'

'I'm sorry.' Biting her lip, she withdrew. 'I'll come back later, okay?'

Niko didn't respond. Iolanthe turned to Alekos and motioned for them both to go out of the room.

Alekos waited until they were back downstairs before he asked the question that was burning in his chest. 'What's wrong with him?'

'Don't *say* that.' Iolanthe whirled around, her expression savage, her voice a crack of a whip that he hadn't expected. Alekos blinked with the force of its sting.

'I'm sorry. I didn't mean...'

'Yes, you did,' she stated flatly. 'Do you know how often I get that question? How people look at him?' She drew a ragged breath and he realised she was near tears. He felt suddenly, overwhelmingly repentant.

'Iolanthe—'

'Don't.' She flung out one hand as if to keep him distant, even though he hadn't moved. 'Don't ask what's wrong with him, don't assume he's rude or badly behaved or whatever else I could see in your face. You looked... disgusted.' Her voice trembled on the word.

'I wasn't,' Alekos said quietly. He felt the stirrings of shame. 'Surprised and disappointed, perhaps. I suppose, unrealistically, I was expecting for a better meeting. Interest, friendship.' Politeness, at least. 'I still don't understand.'

Iolanthe tucked some stray tendrils of hair behind her ears and drew a calming breath. She seemed more composed, resolute, although her face was still pale. 'I told you he was different.'

'I know, but I don't understand why or what that means.'

'The truth is no one really understands,' she admitted on a sigh. 'He's been to a whole raft of doctors and psychiatrists and therapists over the years. They've all had different diagnoses, but none of them really fit.'

'So you knew there was some issue for a while.'

'Yes, since he was small. Even as a baby...he had trouble attaching—breastfeeding was impossible, and he never liked hugs or cuddles. He screamed for the first three months of his life, non-stop.' She spoke tonelessly, reciting these facts as if they didn't matter to her, and yet Alekos knew they had to have cut her deeply.

'And later?' he asked.

Iolanthe let out a deep sigh and sank onto a sofa, her head bowed so Alekos could see the tender nape of her neck. He had the impulse to rest his hand there, rub the muscles he could see corded with tension. He didn't move.

'Similar things. He went to nursery for a short while, but he found it too overwhelming, and he fought with the other children.' She gave a little shake of her head, lost in memory. 'Forming friendships has always been difficult for him. Not impossible—by that time I'd started attending therapy with him, trying to figure out what was wrong and how to help him. Having a routine made things easier and, as he grew older, coaching him in ways to behave that weren't rude or aggressive.' She looked up at him, her eyes shining and damp. 'He's come a long way, Alekos, even if it doesn't seem like it to you.'

'I wouldn't make such a judgment.'

'You already did.' She spoke wearily, without accusation, but even so Alekos felt a sharp pang of guilt.

'I'm sorry. I shouldn't have phrased it like that.'

'You wouldn't be the first. And I'm sorry too. I shouldn't take my frustrations out on you. It's just that this kind of thing has been happening for so long.'

'I understand.' Iolanthe gave him a small, grateful smile that pierced Alekos to the heart. She was thankful for that negligible bit of grace? And yet he realised that they were actually having a civilised conversation. An *important* conversation. Standing there, seeing Iolanthe look so tired and disheartened, Alekos realised there were things he could not begin to fathom about her life.

'Tell me more,' he said, and moved to sit across from her.

'What more do you want to know?'

'I don't know. Anything.' He shrugged, spreading his hands. 'I want to understand.'

She pressed her lips together, her gaze distant. 'Doctors suggested he was on the autism spectrum, but not all of his symptoms fit the classic diagnosis. Of course there's a range, but they weren't entirely comfortable with it and neither was I. Other doctors suggested a sensory disorder, but some of his emotional behaviours didn't fit that either.' She raised her slight shoulders in a helpless shrug. 'In the end they slapped the PDD label on him and called it a day.'

'PDD?'

'Pervasive Developmental Disorder. A jack-of-all-trades diagnosis.' Her smile was wan, heartbreaking. 'We've both coped as best as we can. Taking him out of school helped—it was too much pressure on him to make friends, to behave a certain way. He gets along very well with his tutor.'

'Where is his tutor? I thought he was going to be here this morning.'

'I had him leave early, in anticipation of this meeting.'

Alekos frowned. 'Is that a good idea? If routine is important—'

'Don't question me please, Alekos.' Iolanthe's voice rose sharply. 'I know you like to be in control. I know you want to be the one giving the orders. But please, *please* trust that I might have a better idea of how to handle my son than you do.'

'*Our* son, and only because I was kept from being involved in his life until now,' Alekos returned before he could keep himself from it. Iolanthe flinched.

'Will you always throw that in my face?' she asked quietly.

'No.' He let out a low breath. 'But it's a hard thing to accept, Iolanthe. To forgive.'

'So you've said.' She drew herself up, a new resolve entering her eyes. 'So surely you can see there is no sense in us marrying. We would be at cross purposes all the time, arguing and throwing old hurts in each other's faces.'

'I would hope we are both mature enough not to act in such a way.'

'It wouldn't be a good environment for Niko,' Iolanthe persisted. 'He picks up on such undercurrents. Tension affects him very badly.'

Alekos held on to his temper, keeping his voice both level and firm. 'Then we will both have to make a concerted effort not to have such tension in our home.'

Iolanthe let out a hollow laugh, falling back against the sofa with a weary shake of her head. 'Talking to you is like battering a brick wall. The only thing that happens is I get tired and bruised.'

'Perhaps you need to stop treating our conversations as battles,' Alekos suggested. Iolanthe rolled her eyes.

'It's my fault, then, is it? Of course. Some things never change.' Bitterness spiked her words, making him wonder. Admittedly, the history between them was fraught, but surely they didn't have so much for her to speak with such cynical experience? No matter that they'd created a child together, they still hardly knew one another.

'I don't mean to apportion blame. But I believe strongly indeed that a child belongs with his parents, Iolanthe. *Both* his parents.' Alekos heard the throb of emotion in his voice and inwardly cringed at it. He hated revealing such things.

Iolanthe eyed him with tired curiosity. 'It almost sounds as if you speak from experience.'

'I do.' This time Alekos kept his voice diffident. 'My father left when I was young and I was separated from my mother soon after.'

'I'm sorry.' Her expression had softened into sadness, or maybe pity, which he couldn't stand. 'That must have been very hard.'

'It was what it was.' Alekos dismissed his miserable

childhood with a flick of his shoulders. 'But I do not want the same for Niko.'

'He doesn't do well with a disturbance in his routines, Alekos—'

'And that is your justification for keeping his father out of his life?' he demanded. 'Routines have to be altered, Iolanthe. It is a fact of life. You can't keep Niko up there in his ivory tower for ever.'

'You don't know—'

'Maybe I know more than you think. Maybe I understand some of what Niko is going through—'

'You do?' She looked and sounded disbelieving.

'He is my son. And he grew up with a man who was not his father, as I did.' A sudden suspicion assailed him. 'Was Callos close to him?'

Iolanthe's expression shuttered and she looked away. 'He…he tried,' she said in a low voice.

'He tried? What does that mean?'

'He knew Niko wasn't his biological son…' The words were a wretched whisper, cementing Alekos's suspicions and making fury surge through his blood.

'He knew that when you wed. He never should have married you if he couldn't treat Niko as his own.' He'd thought he hated Lukas Callos already, but he realised he'd barely plumbed the depths of his derision for a man who stole other people's ideas as well as their sons—and failed in both regards.

'Perhaps he thought he could.' Iolanthe's voice was thready. 'I can't blame him…'

'Why not?'

'Because he married me when he knew what I'd done,' Iolanthe stated starkly. 'Which was more than anyone else was willing to do.'

Guilt felt like acid corroding his veins. 'You had sex,' Alekos stated. 'Hardly unforgivable in the twenty-first century.'

'Unforgivable in the world I live in,' Iolanthe returned. 'No matter how the rest of the world sees it.' She sighed and then steeled herself. 'But we were talking about Niko.'

'I want to spend more time with him.' Even as he said the words, Alekos knew that carefully orchestrated visits to Iolanthe's house would not suffice. He needed an environment where he could get to know Niko properly, completely—and, he realised, get to know Iolanthe as well. If he really intended to marry her, for Niko's sake it couldn't be the cold-blooded arrangement he'd initially intended. What it could be, he had no idea, but he needed time to figure it out. They all needed time...as a family. To become the family they could be, the family Alekos had been denied as a child himself, and Niko had too.

'Let's go away,' he said, and Iolanthe's eyes rounded, her lovely mouth dropping open in shock. 'The three of us. Somewhere we can be alone and private together. It will give Niko time to get to know me, and also time for us to know each other and decide if we can make something of a marriage.' He had no intention of allowing Iolanthe to make that decision by herself—it was far too important to leave to emotion or chance. But perhaps a few weeks alone together would remind Iolanthe of what they'd had together.

The spark was still there, Alekos had felt it last night, when he'd brushed by Iolanthe, the softness of her breast touching his arm. He felt it now, leaping between them even as they argued. All he needed to do was fan it into burning flame. Passion was surely a good basis for marriage. Better than slippery, untrustworthy love.

'I told you, Niko doesn't—'

'Do well with a change in routine. Yes. But he must have had holidays.'

Iolanthe shook her head. 'We don't go anywhere.'

His assumption that she had lived a spoilt, carefree socialite's life experienced another blow. 'Then you don't know if a holiday would suit him,' he stated, determined to press his point—and win. 'Give us this chance, Iolanthe. Surely I deserve that much.'

Guilt flashed across her features and her shoulders sagged. 'Very well,' she whispered, and Alekos felt a surge of triumph as well as one of anticipation and desire. He had no intention of letting Iolanthe or his son slip away from him again.

CHAPTER NINE

IOLANTHE LEANED FORWARD, her hands on the railing of Alekos's super yacht, and lifted her face to the sea breeze. She'd been dreading these next few weeks with Alekos, not only for Niko's sake, as he would naturally resist any change, but for her own. A few weeks in Alekos's company and her resolve to be strong and independent would start to crack and crumble. She felt it. She knew it.

Still, she found she was enjoying this moment, with the sun warm on her head and the sea air cool on her face. The Aegean stretched before them in an undulating blanket of blue-green; Alekos had told them his private island was a few hours' sail from the mainland.

Niko had been surprisingly adaptable, if a bit wary, about this sudden holiday. He sat now under an awning on the deck, his laptop opened on the table before him as he worked on another app.

Iolanthe watched out of the corner of her eye as Alekos approached him, his manner relaxed and easy. Out here on the sea, the wind ruffling his dark hair, his skin looking bronzed under the hot Greek sun, Alekos seemed just as formidable and attractive as he did in his office in Athens, dressed in an immaculate suit. Now he wore board shorts and a white T-shirt that the wind whipped against his chest, outlining his pectoral muscles and reminding Iolanthe of how she'd once stroked and touched his chest. She'd called him exquisite.

The memory made her cringe even as a treacherous heat flooded through her. Ten years on Alekos was just as devastatingly sexy, if not more, than he had been back when she'd been a starstruck innocent.

She tried now not to eavesdrop on his conversation with Niko, and in truth there wasn't much to overhear. Alekos's relaxed questions were met with tense, monosyllabic answers, her son's gaze not moving from the computer screen.

Maybe she shouldn't have allowed Niko to bring his laptop, but she knew it acted as a security blanket for him, as well as a confidence-booster. Away from his computer Niko was a socially awkward and uncertain child. In cyberspace, designing apps and interacting online, he was a boy genius.

Alekos left Niko to his laptop and joined her at the deck, making all of Iolanthe's senses go on high alert. She watched out of the corner of her eye as he rested his hands on the railing—strong brown hands that she remembered the feel of against her skin.

'This is all amazing,' she murmured as she looked away. 'A yacht…a private island…' From the moment Alekos had picked them up that morning, she and Niko had experienced unprecedented luxury, from the stretch limo outfitted with video screens and a minibar to the super yacht they were now taking to Alekos's own private paradise. Iolanthe suspected the unaccustomed treats were what was smoothing Niko's transition from comfortable, secure routine into the unknown. So far he'd been surprisingly, quietly amenable to everything, although Iolanthe knew better than to coast along, assuming that was how it was always going to be. Still, she was enjoying the brief reprieve.

'I thought you were used to luxury,' Alekos remarked. 'As the only child of a very rich man and then the wife of another very rich man.'

'Lukas wasn't as rich as all that,' Iolanthe said before she could stop herself. Alekos frowned.

'What do you mean?'

'It doesn't matter,' she dismissed. She didn't want to enlighten Alekos on the sorry state of her financial affairs.

'In any case, I never travelled or experienced this kind of luxury. Not,' she amended, 'that I'm a poor little rich girl, crying over what I didn't have. The country estate I grew up on was very well appointed.'

'And you stayed there your whole childhood?'

'Yes, except for the occasional trip into Athens. My father wanted to keep me sheltered.' Her mouth twisted. 'He was a very old-fashioned man.'

'Do you miss him?' Alekos asked, and Iolanthe heard a note in his tone that she couldn't quite decipher. She didn't think she liked it.

'Yes, although sometimes I think I miss what we could have had if...if things had been different.'

'You mean if we...' He gestured between them, and then to Niko.

'Yes.' She bit her lip. 'He was so angry and disappointed in me, and I'm not sure I can even blame him. But even though I disappointed him, he loved Niko.' She smiled at her son bent over his laptop. 'For that alone I can't hold anything against him. And Niko adored my father.' Talos's admittedly sporadic attention had been a balm after Lukas's continuous rejection. 'His death affected him badly.'

Alekos didn't say anything for a moment, his hooded gaze remaining on the sea. 'Your mother died when you were young,' he stated finally.

'Yes.' She slanted him a questioning glance. 'How did you know that?'

'I read it in a business journal.' His mouth twisted. '"Talos Petrakis the Family Man".'

'He was a family man,' she defended. Now she really didn't like his tone. 'Just a very traditional one.' And she'd chafed against the bonds of duty her father had put on her. Still, she didn't want Alekos criticising him, for Niko's sake if not her own.

Alekos nodded, shifting restlessly, his hands tightening on the railing. 'Of course.' He didn't sound as if he believed her. 'Anyway, it must have been difficult to grow up without a mother.'

'I never knew anything else.' She glanced at him, trying to assess his mood. He'd seemed relaxed when he'd first joined her at the railing, but now he looked tense. 'From what you said the other night, it seems like you grew up with neither.'

'That's correct.' He made it sound as if she'd got a right answer on a maths test.

'It must have been very hard for you,' Iolanthe persisted. Having this conversation made her realise how little she knew this man—and how much she now wanted to. Understanding him a bit better could only help their dealings with each other...whatever those ended up being.

'It was what it was,' Alekos answered, squinting as he looked out at the glittering horizon.

'You said that before, but it doesn't really mean anything.' Alekos just shrugged. Clearly he didn't like talking about himself, or at least about his childhood. She decided to change the subject. 'Did you make some headway with Niko?'

'A beginning. He seems wary of me. Distrustful, even.'

'He's wary of everyone. You shouldn't take it personally.'

Alekos nodded slowly, but the answer didn't seem to satisfy him. With a sinking feeling Iolanthe wondered if Alekos would be on a mission to change Niko or try to fix him. She wanted Alekos to accept and even love their son for who he was, but she knew that would take time.

'So tell me where we're going,' she said, injecting a note of brightness into her voice. 'I heard "private island" but not much else.'

Alekos turned to her with a smiling glance, and for a few seconds Iolanthe could only blink under that topaz gaze. It had her tumbling back ten years, preening shyly under his masculine admiration. She had to remind herself that the situation was very different. *She* was different.

'I suppose one private island in the Aegean is quite like another,' he said with a little laugh.

'I wouldn't know.'

His smiling glance morphed into a frown of surprise. 'You've been on Callos's island, haven't you?'

'No. It was for business only. Entertaining clients, that sort of thing. It used to belong to my father, and he gave it to Lukas before he died. But it was never meant to be a family home.'

Alekos's frown deepened. 'But it was in your family for generations.'

'You seem to know a great deal about my family,' Iolanthe returned, her voice coming out a little more sharply than she'd intended.

'Not as much as I thought.' Alekos's gaze rested on her thoughtfully, and Iolanthe's mouth twisted wryly.

'You thought I was a spoiled princess.' She sighed as she stared out at the shimmering sea. 'I suppose in some ways I was. My father was strict but growing up in the country I had plenty of freedom and luxury, lonely as it was. But since marrying Lukas…' She pressed her lips together, not wanting to mention her marriage. The un-happiness that had burrowed deeper and deeper, a canker that by the end had poisoned everything.

'You weren't happy in your marriage,' Alekos stated quietly, and wordlessly Iolanthe shook her head. She didn't trust herself to say anything more.

Alekos rested his hand over hers on the railing, the contact jolting her right down to her toes. 'This is a new start, Iolanthe. It can be. For all of us.'

She looked up at him, achingly conscious of the feel of his skin on hers. 'Do you need a new start?'

'I want to have one with you and Niko.'

Too unsettled by his surprising honesty to reply,

Iolanthe slid her hand out from under his. 'I should go check on Niko.'

Alekos glanced back at Niko, who was still immersed in his laptop. 'He's fine—'

Iolanthe didn't answer, just hurried towards her son. What did Alekos mean, a new start for all of them? What was he envisioning? When he'd first proposed marriage, Iolanthe had envisioned a loveless union created for expediency's sake. Just as her marriage to Lukas had been.

But for a moment, with Alekos's hand on hers, she'd felt as if he'd been suggesting something else. Something more, something that harked back to that first magical night. And some desperate part of her soul longed for that.

'How's the app?' Iolanthe asked as she slid on the bench across from Niko. 'Still tracking zombies?'

Niko gave a little shake of his head. 'I finished that one.'

'What do you do with your apps, Niko?' Iolanthe didn't really understand the world her son inhabited, of online gaming and mobile apps and the rest of it. She barely used her mobile phone; she had few friends to call. Caring for Niko and being married to Lukas had completely limited her social interactions.

Niko shrugged. 'Nothing much. Show them to some people online.'

'Maybe you could market them,' Iolanthe suggested. 'Sell them through Petra Innovation.'

Niko hunched his shoulders, shooting her a dark look before looking away. 'Father wasn't interested in them.'

A lump rose in her throat, which she swallowed down. 'I'm interested in them, Niko.' Except she might not have a Petra Innovation to help develop her son's interests and ambitions. 'Alekos might be interested in them,' she added. 'Why don't you show them to him?'

Niko shot one look at Alekos, still standing at the rail, and shook his head. 'No.'

Iolanthe decided not to press. She knew that Niko was

afraid of rejection, just as she was. Alekos might be whisking them away to his private island, but Iolanthe still didn't trust what he wanted from them in the long term. What if, after a few days, he grew tired of them? Impatient with Niko's quirks and bored of her? He'd certainly bored of her quickly the last time they'd spent any time together.

Trying to ignore the nerves now churning in her stomach, Iolanthe smiled at Niko and left him to his laptop. She'd brought a book but she didn't feel as if she could concentrate to read. She closed her eyes instead, trying to enjoy the sun on her face and simply be.

She must have dozed off without realising because the next thing she knew Alekos was standing in front of her, blocking the sun, a hand on her shoulder. 'You'll get sunburned.'

Her eyes fluttered open and she stared at him dazedly. With the sun behind him he looked dark and tall, forbidding and sexy. She pressed one hand to her cheek, shaking her head to try to clear the cobwebs. 'I'm under the awning.'

'The sun's moved.' Alekos cocked his head. 'You're going to have a red stripe down your face if you're not careful.'

'I put sun cream on,' Iolanthe said as she moved farther under the awning. She didn't relish the thought of sporting a ridiculous-looking sunburn.

'Lunch will be ready in a few minutes,' Alekos said as he slid onto the bench next to hers. His thigh nudged hers and Iolanthe felt her senses see-saw crazily from just that brief contact. She froze, unsure whether to inch away from him or act as if she hadn't noticed.

'When will we arrive at the island?'

'Another hour or so.' He turned a smiling glance on his son. 'Still surfing the Internet, Niko?' He spoke lightly but Iolanthe could see the worry in his eyes, feel it in the taut length of muscle next to her leg. He wanted to bond with Niko.

'Yeah.' Niko ducked his head, not looking at Alekos, and Iolanthe knew he didn't want to tell Alekos about the apps because he didn't want to risk scorn or derision. Lukas's silent rejection of her child ran deep.

The member of Alekos's staff who had been discreetly seeing to their needs on the yacht now called them to the aft deck where a table and chairs had been brought out, set for what looked like a lavish lunch.

'This is amazing,' Iolanthe murmured as Alekos pulled out her chair. She surveyed the spread of different pitas and dips, several fresh salads and a tray of roasted meat with appreciation.

'Dig in,' Alekos said lightly as he popped the cork on a bottle of sparkling wine and poured Iolanthe a very full glass.

She gave an uncertain laugh. 'It's the middle of the afternoon...'

'We're celebrating.' Alekos's eyes met hers, and she saw both heat and expectation in their tawny depths. The knowledge that he still desired her, that something might actually happen between them again, sent alarm bells jangling in her head and heat pooling low in her belly.

'Why not?' she murmured, and took the glass of bubbly from him.

Alekos sat opposite and served everyone from the different dishes, asking Niko what he preferred, keeping the conversation light and easy. Iolanthe watched out of the corner of her eye as the tension that had kept her son's slight body rigid slowly eased. He didn't talk much and he only picked at his food, but it was progress.

After they'd eaten Niko went to sit farther on the aft deck, facing the sea, watching the water churn and foam as the yacht cut smoothly through the water.

Iolanthe watched him with wry pleasure. 'You've managed to pry him off his laptop.'

'I think it's most likely the surroundings rather than me,' Alekos answered, topping up both of their glasses and leaning back in his chair.

Iolanthe already felt pleasantly relaxed and slightly muddle-headed from the wine. After the near-constant levels of stress of the last few months—or years, if she was honest—it felt rather wonderful.

And the surroundings Niko was currently enjoying *were* incredible—azure sky, lemon-yellow sun, and sparkling aquamarine water in every direction. 'Still, it's a blessing,' she said as she took a sip of the sparkling wine. It was crisp and bubbly on her tongue. 'And I've learned not to take those for granted.' She spoke the words unthinkingly, too relaxed to guard her tongue, and Alekos swept her with a considering gaze.

'How have you learned that, Iolanthe?'

Something about the way he said her name, taking his time with the syllables, made a tremor go through her. Just seeing him there sprawled in his chair, the T-shirt moulded to his chest and the board shorts emphasising his long, muscular legs, the wind ruffling his dark hair, caused another tremor. He was so *beautiful*, with his bronze skin and topaz eyes and air of utter masculine authority. Her gaze fell to his fingers cradling his wine glass and she remembered what those fingers had felt like on her body, touching her in secret places. Quickly she looked away.

'I suppose it's called growing up,' she said with a wry smile. 'Happens to everybody.'

'Maybe,' Alekos allowed. 'But some people have to grow up more quickly than others.'

'Like you did?' She'd rather talk about him than herself, and in truth she was curious about his past and the few references he'd made to it.

'Yes, I suppose I had to grow up fast,' Alekos said. His voice was measured, a little wary.

'Tell me,' Iolanthe said. 'Considering our…situation, we should get to know more about one another.'

Alekos looked as if he was about to resist but then he caught sight of Niko gazing out at the water and he said, reluctance audible in his voice, 'What do you want to know?'

'You said you lost both your parents when you were young.'

A terse nod. 'My father left when I was four years old.'

'You mean…he just walked out?'

'That's exactly what I mean.' Alekos shrugged, rotating his glass between his fingers as he gazed down into its swirling depths. 'Plenty of men shirk their responsibilities to their families. I never intend to be one of them.'

Guilt assailed her then, as piercing and accurate as an arrow. 'That's what you said…' she began, and Alekos's gaze narrowed.

'When?'

'Then. That night.' And just like that the memory of that evening seemed to shimmer in the air between them, and Iolanthe felt her limbs tremble with weakness as desire flooded through her. How could it still be so strong, after all these years? After all the sadness? But maybe her reaction to Alekos was simply because she hadn't felt desire or experienced male attention for a long, long time. For the entire length of her marriage.

'Yes, I did say that then,' Alekos said. His gaze was trained on hers, seeking, burning. 'And I meant it.'

'I'm sorry,' she said quietly. 'I hadn't realised about your past…'

He shook his head. 'I didn't tell you. And the truth is…' He glanced down at his glass again, his expression shadowed. 'I didn't act charitably towards you then. That night or after.'

Iolanthe could feel her heart bumping in her chest. She'd

never expected Alekos, so cold and arrogant and unyielding, to admit even that much. Deciding the mood needed
to be lightened, she gave him a small, wry smile. 'Wait,
was that actually an apology?'

He smiled back, slow and sensual, making her senses
somersault. 'Something like it.'

'I'll take it. Thank you.' She took a deep breath. 'And
I didn't act charitably towards you in keeping my pregnancy from you. I'm sorry.'

'Apology accepted.'

Was it that easy? They'd said their apologies, they
could draw a line across the past, and start afresh? Did she
even want that? Confused by her own muddled feelings,
Iolanthe took another sip of wine, gazing out at the horizon to keep from looking at Alekos with what she feared
might be hunger in her eyes.

Being here with him like this, when he seemed warm
and approachable and *sexy*, brought back too many memories. Wonderful memories, and other, awful ones corroded
by confusion and hurt. Tangled together, they made her
more uncertain than ever, not knowing how to feel.

'You mentioned that you lost your mother soon after...?'

Alekos shifted in his seat. 'My mother did the best she
could, but she couldn't manage all of us.'

'All of you?'

'I had—have—three siblings. We were separated when
I was six, to various distant relatives or foster families.'

Iolanthe stared at him, appalled. 'They couldn't keep
you together?'

'No one had the money or resources to care for four
children.'

'But that's terrible.' Iolanthe shook her head slowly.
'Where did you go?'

'A foster family. They were nice enough, kept me
clothed and fed, made sure I got to school.' But loveless,

Iolanthe surmised. Alekos had grown up without love or affection.

'And your siblings?'

'We lost touch over the years. The social workers tried at first, but it's all too easy for kids to slip through the cracks, and my mother died when I was ten, which made us even more lost in the system.' He sighed, rotating his glass between his fingers. 'One of my sisters was adopted, and my brother got into trouble with the law. Beyond that...' He shrugged, letting the words trickle away.

'You mean you don't know what happened to them? You never found out?'

'No.' Alekos's voice was hard. 'I never tried too hard because I suspected they didn't want to be found. They could have found me just as easily.'

'But that's so sad.' A lump formed in her throat. No wonder Alekos was so determined to be a good father to Niko. 'I'm sorry.'

He shrugged. 'I've moved on.'

But did anyone move on from that kind of sadness? Iolanthe decided they needed to lighten the mood. She cleared her throat and took another sip of wine. 'When are we going to get to this private island of yours?'

'We're almost there.' Alekos rose from his chair in one fluid movement. Iolanthe had the sense that he was as discomfited by their conversation as she was. 'Look.' He reached for her hand and Iolanthe enjoyed the sensation of his fingers sliding along hers as he drew her up to join Niko at the bow of the yacht. 'Do you see that blur of green on the horizon?' he asked them both.

Iolanthe squinted as she gazed out at the sea. 'Yes...is that your island? It looks rather big.'

'A few square miles.'

'Wow.' Impressed, she watched as the strip of green came closer, and soon she and Niko could make out rocky outcroppings, the twisted trunks of olive trees, and a lovely white strip of sandy beach.

Alekos Demetriou was a successful man, Iolanthe acknowledged afresh, as the yacht was guided towards the dock. A rich man. Above them a sprawling villa of white stone, its many windows possessing wrought-iron balconies that overflowed with pots of trailing bougainvillea, perched with views of the sea in every direction.

Now that they were about to get off the yacht, Niko had started acting nervous of the next step. Iolanthe could hardly blame him; she was as well. She touched his shoulder lightly, a second's reassurance, and he shrugged away and jammed his hands into the pockets of his shorts, hunching his shoulders.

Alekos noticed the change in his son and thankfully took it in his stride. 'Why don't you and your mother have a look round the villa?' he suggested. 'You can choose what bedrooms you like. My staff will deal with the luggage.'

Grateful for his understanding that their son might need a bit of space, Iolanthe stepped off the yacht and started up the steps that had been carved into the rock face. Niko followed her, gazing around with wide, wary eyes.

A housekeeper was waiting at the front door as they approached; she must have been prepped by Alekos because besides offering them a welcome and inviting them in, she left them to it. The villa's foyer was huge and airy, with skylights that let in the bright sunshine and a double staircase that led to the first floor.

Iolanthe glanced at Niko. 'What do you want to look at first?'

Niko nodded towards the stairs and, feeling a mixture of trepidation and excitement for this new adventure, Iolanthe started up them with her son.

CHAPTER TEN

THE SUN WAS just starting to sink towards the placid sea as Alekos stepped out on the private balcony from the master bedroom and released his breath in a frustrated rush.

He'd left Iolanthe and Niko alone for the last few hours, sensing that they would both need time to settle in without his interference. He'd watched them from afar an hour ago as they'd left the villa and explored the pool and garden; he'd heard Iolanthe's laughter, that throaty husk that he remembered from ten years ago and still had the power to make his body stir insistently.

The whole day had felt like an endurance test, watching Iolanthe, seeing how she relaxed, her silvery eyes lighting from within. She'd worn a simple strappy sundress that highlighted her smooth skin and slender curves and had made Alekos's hands itch to touch her.

They still itched. And although he'd told himself they would take it slow, considering she was recently bereaved, his body was insisting otherwise. She was the mother of his child. She was going to be his wife. And the chemistry between them, as far as he could tell, was as electric and overwhelming as ever. Why shouldn't they enjoy each other?

He'd arranged for a private dinner out on the terrace, after Niko had gone to bed. Now he found he couldn't wait to be alone with Iolanthe, even as a restless dissatisfaction gnawed at him. Not just a sexual need repressed—heaven knew, he certainly felt that. But a dissatisfaction that he was up here alone, pacing his room like a leashed tiger, while his son and his wife-to-be spent time alone, away from him, because he was not yet part of their circle. They weren't yet a family.

Which was why they'd come here, Alekos reminded himself. He simply needed to be patient.

Yet no matter what apology of Iolanthe's he'd accepted, the injustice still burned. He knew what it was like to be on the fringes of a family, to feel as if he didn't belong and never would. He'd felt it his entire childhood, knowing full well he was a duty to be dealt with to his foster family and nothing more.

They'd never been remiss in their care of him, but a thousand tiny slights had made him all too aware that this was not his family and never would be. There had been no birthday parties, no special treats, no hugs or chats at bedtime like there were with his foster siblings. He'd felt every lack even as he'd come to expect them. He'd vowed to leave them as soon as he could, and when he had he'd known they'd been as relieved as he was. Looking back, he could understand it a little bit better—he'd been a sullen, studious child, often silent and surly, refusing to be won over. Not that they'd tried. But he'd hated feeling like an outsider then, and he despised it even more now, feeling it as an adult with his own child—and all because Iolanthe had kept the truth from him. He'd told her that her deception was hard to forgive, and he'd meant it. He couldn't let it go even now, even though he wanted to.

Alekos drew a deep breath and let it out slowly. He could see Iolanthe and Niko making their way around the infinity pool towards the villa. He'd be with her soon enough. He'd have her soon enough, and perhaps then this restlessness would finally leave him.

An hour later the shadows were lengthening on the terrace, cast by flickering citronella candles, when Iolanthe stepped through the French windows to join Alekos.

He turned, taking in the sight of her slowly, savouring the way she moved, her dress whispering about her legs.

She'd changed into a slightly more formal dress made of ecru cotton and lace, the material sheer enough for him to see the camisole she wore underneath. She'd left her hair loose, dark and wavy about her shoulders, and Alekos didn't think he'd ever seen her look so beautiful.

More beautiful even than she'd been at twenty, young and girlish and innocent. Now she was a woman, her face a little more lined, experience reflected in her eyes, and he realised he was more attracted to her now than he'd been back then.

'How is Niko?' he asked as he handed her a glass of *agiorgitiko.*

'I just tucked him in. He's tired from all the activity.' She took a sip of her drink, her eyes widening as she tasted it. 'What is this?'

'*Agiorgitiko.* A mix of fruit juice, rum, and red wine. An island speciality.'

'It's delicious.' She took another sip, her eyes smiling at him from over the rim of her glass, making him want to snatch her up and kiss the wine from her lips. 'Thank you. This is all really amazing.' Her nod encompassed the entire island: villa, pool, gardens, and rocky beaches beyond. 'I think it will be good for Niko to be here. We may have got in a bit of a rut back in Athens.'

'How so?' Alekos asked. He placed a hand low on her back and guided her towards the railing that overlooked the infinity pool. The placid water shimmered with the first starlight.

Iolanthe was silent for a moment, marshalling her thoughts. Alekos kept his hand on her back, enjoying the warm feel of her, the slight tremor of awareness he could feel twanging through her at his touch.

'Everything seemed so difficult,' she said after a moment. 'Struggles with Niko...and with Lukas.' She bit her lip as if she regretted saying so much, and Alekos felt a surge of both jealousy and protectiveness. He hated the thought of Iolanthe with Lukas, but he realised he hated the thought of her unhappy with him even more. 'It was easier simply not to go out,' she explained. 'Niko was tutored at home, and Lukas was always at work. I didn't have many friends or social engagements.' She gave a little shrug, her mouth turning down at the corners. 'I think perhaps it would have been better for Niko and me to get out more. Take him out of his shell. Both of us, really.'

'But you said school was difficult for him.'

'Yes, but he likes other things. Swimming, for one. I used to take him swimming at the community pool, if it wasn't too crowded. He's looking forward to jumping in there tomorrow.' She nodded towards the infinity pool. 'And museums. He loves studying things, memorising facts about them. We visited the Natural History Museum in Kifisia when he was little. I'm not sure when we stopped going.' She sighed, remorse creasing her eyes and making her frown. 'Somehow it just all became too much.'

'I'm glad, then, that this is providing something new for Niko.' He paused, wanting to lighten her expression. 'And for you.' Another pause as he considered how to frame his thoughts. 'It doesn't seem as if the last ten years have been very happy for you.'

Her gaze flew to his and then away again. She took a sip of her drink, an inner struggle evident on her face. 'I've learned to be content,' she said at last.

'That doesn't sound very encouraging.'

Iolanthe gave a little shrug. 'Like you said, it is what it is. I knew going into my marriage that it wouldn't be a love match.'

'Why did Callos marry you?' Alekos asked, trying to keep the question level when inside he felt a tormented tangle of too many feelings. 'Was it really just to cement his position at your father's company?'

'Yes. He had no affection for me, I can assure you.'

'And why did you marry him?'

Disbelief and an unsettling contempt curled her mouth. 'Can you really ask that, Alekos? I was pregnant.'

'I would have married you,' he confessed in a low voice. 'If you'd just told me the truth...'

'So it's back to blaming me?' she finished. 'You never said as much, you know. You simply told me you would take care of your responsibilities. How did I know what that meant? Maybe you intended to pay for my abortion.'

He drew back, shocked and deeply insulted. 'I would have never suggested such a thing.'

'The point is,' Iolanthe returned, 'I didn't know. And the one time I sought you out, you terrified me. You looked like you hated me, Alekos. And my father was insisting on the marriage. I felt like I had no choice...' Her voice caught and she blinked rapidly, looking away. 'You have no idea what it was like.'

'Iolanthe...' Regret lashed him and he put his hand on her arm. Iolanthe shrugged him away.

'I should have never put you in that position,' Alekos said in a low voice. He'd been so angry when he'd seen her back then, but it had been anger at her father's unjust treatment. He shouldn't have taken it out on her.

'I'm not sure why we're talking about this,' Iolanthe said. 'I thought we said our apologies earlier.'

'We did, but a simple apology doesn't erase a decade of pain and sadness. It's hard to let go of these old hurts.'

'Hard for you,' Iolanthe clarified. 'You can't forgive me, can you? For not telling you about Niko.' She stared at him with the same fragile, open honesty she'd had in her eyes when he'd met her ten years ago. Alekos looked away.

How could he answer her? Forgiveness was not part of his nature. He'd held on to his grievances against Talos Petrakis because they defined him. Revenge had always been his goal, his lodestone. He wasn't sure he knew how to change.

'Your silence says it all,' Iolanthe answered with a re-signed sigh.

'I'm still coming to terms with all of this,' Alekos answered. He took a deep breath, needing to ask the next question even if the answer hurt him. 'Was Lukas...was he a good father to Niko?'

Iolanthe was silent for so long that Alekos tensed to hear her answer, dread pooling in his stomach. 'I think he tried at first,' she finally said. 'He tried to try, anyway. But...'

Alekos tensed further, knowing he both didn't want and needed to hear this. 'But what?' he asked, his voice coming out in a near-growl.

'He never bonded with him,' Iolanthe admitted quietly. 'He might have tried a little at the very beginning, but, as I said before, Niko was a difficult baby. He had colic, and Lukas couldn't handle the constant crying. He withdrew from both of us, sleeping in the corporate flat most nights.'

Alekos waited a moment, not trusting himself to sound calm. 'And later? When Niko wasn't a baby?'

'He couldn't get over that Niko wasn't his son,' Iolanthe admitted in a whisper. 'He started blanking him out, ignoring him as often as he could, just as he did me. Niko tried to reach him at first. They both loved computers and technology, and it should have been something they bonded over. But Lukas wouldn't even try. I think his rejection hurt Niko terribly.' A tear slipped down her cheek, splashing onto her thumb. She wiped it away with a shaky laugh. 'I don't know why I'm coming apart now—'

'I wanted you to tell me. I want to know.'

'I feel guilty,' Iolanthe burst out, her voice low and tormented. 'Sometimes I wonder if Niko would have done better with me alone, rather than with a father who had no time for him. If I'd been more confident I wouldn't have married Lukas. I would have struck out on my own, looking for that adventure I once told you about.' She smiled through her tears and it felt like a fist closing around Alekos's heart. 'I wish I had. Maybe then…maybe then Niko wouldn't have the struggles he has now.'

Her voice broke on the last words and Alekos reached for her. 'You can't lose yourself in regret,' he said as he stroked her hair and she nestled against him. 'You have to look towards the future.' The feel of her body pliant against his pushed his self-control to the limit. He longed to tilt her face up towards his, kiss the tears from her cheeks and then plunder her plush mouth. But Iolanthe needed his comfort and compassion now, not his lust.

'I suppose you're right,' she murmured, staying in the shelter of his arms.

It was advice he gave without taking himself, Alekos knew. For fourteen years he'd let the past guide and control him, shaping every action he took, even now. But unlike Iolanthe he had no regrets. Petrakis deserved to have his company destroyed. It had been built on Alekos's hard work, after all. Even now he couldn't let go of that knowledge, that goal. *Especially* now. Talos Petrakis had conspired to take his son from him as well as his business. He could have told Iolanthe the truth about what had happened long ago, could have allowed her to make up her own mind about who to marry.

Are you really going to blame Petrakis for your own failings? You're the one who drove her away. Who told her to leave.

Perhaps Iolanthe felt the new tension in his body for she moved out of his embrace, turning her head away from him. 'It feels strange to be comforted by you.'

Alekos flinched as if he'd been dealt a body blow. 'I suppose it does.'

'I'm not used to depending on anyone.' She turned to face him, her gaze as clear as a full moon. 'I'm afraid of depending on you, Alekos, of Niko depending on you.'

Alekos tried to keep the affront from his voice. 'I won't let you down.'

'That requires a certain level of trust,' Iolanthe answered as her gaze flitted away from his. 'And trust has to be earned…for both of us.'

He hated the thought that she feared he'd fail her. *Again.* 'Which is why we're here. To get to know one another. To learn to trust one another.'

'Yes,' Iolanthe said, but she didn't sound convinced. Ten years was a lot of time to make up for…for both of them.

'Let's eat,' Alekos said, needing to lighten the mood. He took her by the hand and led her to the table that had been laid with crystal and silver and linen; his housekeeper, Eleni, was waiting to bring in the first course.

Iolanthe's grey gaze swept over the table shimmering with candlelight, the bottle of wine chilling in a silver bucket. 'This looks very nice. Very…romantic.' She said the word quickly, her tongue darting out to touch her lips as she shot him a furtive, uncertain glance.

'Why shouldn't we enjoy each other's company? We did once before.'

'That feels like a lifetime ago.'

'Then that is something we need to change,' Alekos answered, and pulled out her chair for her to sit down.

Iolanthe's body felt as if it were twanging with tension. She'd already had the stress of coming away with Alekos, encountering this great unknown, and then Niko, overtired and starting to feel anxious, had been difficult to settle into bed. But this new tension, this frightening yet thrilling sexual energy that zinged between her and Alekos…that was more overwhelming than everything else combined.

She sat down, tensing as he reached for her napkin and placed it in her lap, his fingers brushing her thighs. A pulsing ache began at her centre and she closed her eyes briefly. 'Alekos…'

'Enjoy this evening, Iolanthe.' His voice was a whisper,

a caress of breath against her cheek. 'It seems as if you have had very little to enjoy in your life these last years.'

He moved to the other side of the table and sat down, looking relaxed and assured and positively lethal. How did he make a simple, white button-down shirt, open at the throat, and a pair of black trousers look so sexy? The clothes would have made Lukas look like a waiter, but then Iolanthe knew she couldn't compare her former husband with the man in front of her in any way, shape or form. Alekos outshone Lukas in every way possible.

'My life wasn't quite that grim,' she said as the housekeeper came forward with the first course, an orzo salad with cucumber and feta cheese. 'I have had some happiness, you know.'

'I didn't mean to say you didn't,' Alekos answered. 'But it does sound as if it was limited—whether by choice or necessity.'

Yes, Iolanthe supposed it had been. The town house where she'd lived with Lukas was luxurious enough, but it had been decorated by an interior designer and didn't bear much of Iolanthe's own stamp. And it had been so depressingly empty for so long—just her and Niko rattling around, trying to fill the days.

'I certainly haven't experienced anything like this,' Iolanthe admitted. 'Were you this successful ten years ago?' The question was one of natural curiosity but Alekos frowned as if she'd asked something personal. Iolanthe's insides clenched with nerves. She couldn't stand this seesawing. It was as much to do with her as it was with Alekos; she was too attuned to his moods, too sensitive about their changes. It frightened her, because if she felt this much now, what would happen if she really started to care about Alekos? If she married him?

'No, I wasn't back then,' Alekos answered, jolting Iolanthe out of her thoughts. She was glad to see him looking relaxed again, and it made her relax as well. 'I was just starting out then, really, with my company.'

'Demetriou Tech.'

'Yes.'

'Well, you've obviously worked hard and succeeded amazingly.'

'Success is important to me.'

'Because of your childhood?' Iolanthe surmised, and Alekos's hooded gaze snapped to hers.

'Yes, because of that,' he said, but she had a feeling there was something he wasn't telling her. She supposed there were a lot of things he wasn't telling her; although she'd had glimpses into this complex and fascinating man, she didn't feel she'd yet been granted a true insight. But, as Alekos had said, maybe that was what this time on the island was about...if they could just let go of old hurts and wrongs and try together.

The conversation stayed relatively light for the rest of the delicious meal as they exchanged interests and opinions without delving deeper into the sea of emotion and remembrance that surged beneath them.

'Perhaps you can take up your art again here,' Alekos suggested.

'There's plenty to sketch,' Iolanthe agreed. The prospect of drawing again filled her with a wary anticipation. She'd barely picked up a pencil in ten years. She hadn't had the time or the creative energy, and, she realised, she'd been too unhappy to think of expressing herself in that way. But here...now...a smile curved her mouth at the possibility.

'I can tell that suggestion appeals to you,' Alekos observed with a smile.

The moon had risen high in the sky, sending a lambent shimmer across the sea. The detritus of one of the best meals Iolanthe had ever eaten lay before them, and she was loath to end the evening, although she knew she should check on Niko.

'Thank you,' she said. 'This has been lovely.'

'It has,' Alekos agreed. He rose from the table and walked around to help Iolanthe from her chair. She took his hand, anticipating the sparks of attraction that flared at the touch, but then Alekos pulled her closer to him so their hips nudged and his head tilted down towards her and Iolanthe felt everything in her turn to flame.

'It doesn't have to end now,' Alekos said in a low voice. 'Here.'

She flicked her gaze up to his face, thrilled and alarmed to see the naked lust in his face. He hid nothing.

His gaze dropped to her mouth and Iolanthe's lips parted in helpless response. It had been so long since she'd been kissed.

'You are lovelier than ever,' Alekos murmured, and, just as he had ten years ago, he stroked her cheek with his thumb, making Iolanthe both shiver and yearn. 'So exquisite.'

'You called me that ten years ago,' she whispered. She couldn't look away from his golden gaze. Alekos rested his thumb on her parted lips.

'I remember. You were exquisite then, Iolanthe, and you are even more exquisite now. I want you more now than I did then, which I thought wasn't even possible.'

She let out a shaky laugh, tempted and terrified in turns. 'Alekos, we can't...'

His gaze darkened and his thumb pressed down on her lip, making a tiny indentation. She drew her breath in a gasp of yearning. 'Why can't we?'

'Because it's too soon. Too much,' she said, barely managing to frame the words. 'A few hours ago we were talking about trust. Now you want to sleep with me?'

'Tell me you don't want the same,' Alekos returned, his voice harsh with desire.

'I do,' Iolanthe admitted raggedly. 'Of course I do.' To be touched and treasured again, all her senses waking up with the clarion call of desire…how could she resist? 'But I'm holding on to my sanity by my fingernails, because I know this isn't a good idea.' With what felt like superhuman effort she stepped away from him, out of the range of his touch and heat. 'We need to take our time with this, Alekos. For my sake as well as Niko's. I can't…I can't go through what I did before. Not again.'

Alekos's eyes flashed as he pressed his lips together. 'I won't hurt you, Iolanthe.'

'I'm not sure that's a promise you can make just yet,' she answered on a shaky laugh. Her heart seemed to be beating through her whole body, a drumming tattoo of desperate need. She yearned to take that one step closer to him, lift her face to his, and let him bring them both to the heights she'd experienced only once before. It had been so long, and yet…

The memory of how desolate she'd been kept her standing still. Just.

'When we are married,' Alekos said in a hard voice, 'I expect you to share my bed.'

'When?' The tidal wave of lust started to recede. 'You sound very sure of yourself, Alekos.' As if that was a surprise. 'I thought the point of coming here was to get to know each other better. To help us decide *if* we should get married.'

'No,' Alekos answered without hesitation. 'It was to help us to get to know each other because we are going to marry. I told you, Iolanthe, I don't negotiate.'

CHAPTER ELEVEN

IOLANTHE DREW HERSELF up to rail at Alekos for his high-handed attitude, and then she deflated. She was too tired to engage in yet another battle, and being here was meant to be about building trust, not seeking arguments.

'I'm not going to debate the point with you,' she said with dignity. 'Suffice it to say this is not the Middle Ages, and you can't frogmarch me to the altar.'

A muscle ticced in Alekos's cheek. 'That is hardly something I would ever do. But I thought we'd reached an agreement. What's best for Niko—'

'Has yet to be decided. Now I'm going to bed. Alone,' she added, in case he had any ideas on that score. Alekos's eyes flashed with banked ire and he gave one terse nod. 'Thank you for this lovely dinner,' Iolanthe said. 'And for everything. Being here...' She spread her hands, wanting to defuse Alekos's anger and recapture some of the closeness she'd felt they'd shared earlier. 'Just give me time, Alekos.'

Alekos's expression didn't change. 'It appears I am doing exactly that.'

Sighing, Iolanthe turned and headed for bed.

He couldn't sleep. Alekos lay on the king-sized bed that was most decidedly meant for two, his arms pillowed under his head as he stared up at the ceiling fan turning lazily and catching moonbeams.

The evening hadn't ended as he'd either wanted or expected. Everything had been going so well...when he'd held Iolanthe in his arms, he'd felt her yield to him. She'd wanted him then, for both comfort and satisfaction.

And he wanted to give her both. He wanted her in bed—yes, that was the overwhelming desire he had right now. But over the course of the evening he'd discovered he liked talking to her. He was interested in her ideas and he admired the strength of character she'd developed to survive ten years of an unhappy marriage and come out both swinging and smiling.

Although maybe her marriage hadn't been as unhappy as he'd thought. Jealousy was an uncomfortable emotion, and one he wasn't used to dealing with. And he was jealous on several counts...jealous of Lukas Callos having both the wife and child Alekos should have had all along.

But maybe it's your fault you didn't.

Maybe if he'd been kinder to Iolanthe when she'd come to talk to him, they would have reached an agreement. They would have married. If Talos Petrakis would have even let Iolanthe marry him.

Unease churned inside him. He'd heard the sadness in Iolanthe's voice when she'd talked about Talos. It made it difficult indeed for Alekos to tell her the truth about her father. But if he didn't tell her the truth, Iolanthe would never understand what drove him. How wronged he'd been.

But maybe she didn't need to understand. His business interests were separate from his personal life, and Petra Innovation was finished no matter what. He had no intention of letting his rival's business prosper. His son would inherit his own business, the one he'd built with his two hands, the one with *his* name. He'd be damned if he'd let Talos Petrakis, even from the grave, have anything more of him.

Letting out a long, tired sigh, Alekos closed his eyes and tried to will himself to sleep. Patience. Patience was what he needed now.

He was just starting to settle into sleep when a sudden, keening cry split the still air. Alekos bolted upright, his heart racing at the unholy sound. It came again, sharper and more urgent, and he swung out of bed, groping for a pair of pyjama bottoms and yanking them on before sprinting out into the corridor.

The sound was coming from Niko's room, and as Alekos drew closer he heard Iolanthe's soothing murmurs in reply. The hair on Alekos's nape prickled with alarm as the sounds didn't lessen in their awful urgency.

Gently he pushed open the door, peering inside to see moonlight washing over the two forms on the bed: Niko sitting straight up in bed, his mouth open in a scream of terror, and Iolanthe next to him, her hair like a dark cloud about her face as she spoke soothingly to him.

'What—?' Alekos began and she turned to him, one finger pressed to her lips, her eyes wide and commanding.

Alekos fell silent. Clearly this was a familiar situation to Iolanthe, and that made him feel even more unsettled. What unknown demons did Niko face, to cry like this?

It seemed an age before Niko's sobs finally began to quiet, although in reality Alekos knew it was probably about ten minutes. He watched as Iolanthe gently guided her son to lie down in bed, and then drew the cover up over him, brushing his hair away from his forehead with the tips of her fingers, a sad smile curving her lovely mouth and haunting her eyes.

Niko settled into sleep with a hiccuping sigh, and Iolanthe sat on the edge of the bed for a moment more, her shoulders sagging as if she bore a weight she knew all too well. Then she straightened, lifting her chin, and walked towards Alekos.

'He's asleep now,' she whispered as she moved past him, and Alekos caught the vanilla scent of her hair, saw the modest, yet to him unbearably erotic, nightgown she was wearing—a silk sheath scalloped with lace, the curves of her body caressed by the material.

Alekos closed the door behind him. 'Why was he so upset?' he asked in a low voice.

'Night terrors. He's not even fully awake. There's no way to comfort him, really, you just have to wait it out.'

Alekos stared at her, appalled. 'Night terrors? How often does he have them?'

'They were becoming more infrequent,' Iolanthe answered, a tremble entering her voice, 'until Lukas died. They've come more often since then.'

Alekos frowned as he tried to suppress the rage that crashed over him at the thought of how much his enemy had had of his. How much he'd squandered. 'But I thought Lukas didn't have much of a relationship with him. Does Niko miss him? Is that why…?'

'I don't know. Perhaps it's just the change. Niko's never done well with that. And death is a hard and terrible thing, no matter what.'

Alekos nodded, digesting this, wishing he could change things. 'I hate hearing him cry like that.'

'I know. It tears me apart, but I've become used to it, I suppose.' She lifted her silvery gaze to him. 'It must have been hard for you. I'm sorry.'

The fact that this woman who had endured so much, and much of it because of his own actions, was now comforting him made Alekos struggle to frame a response. He was humbled by her dignity and strength, and he ached to comfort her as she was trying to comfort him. And over all that was an increasingly uncomfortable realisation that he didn't like having all these *feelings*.

'Iolanthe…' he began, and then found he couldn't go on because he felt too much to put it into words, and that alone was enough to terrify him into silence. Iolanthe must have seen something of it in his eyes for her lips parted and she made some movement—Alekos wasn't sure what—but suddenly he was reaching for her, hands curling around her shoulders and then sliding through her hair as his mouth found hers.

He felt no hesitation or reluctance in her embrace, just

acceptance and need. And nothing had felt so right as having Iolanthe in his arms again. He'd waited ten years for this. He just hadn't realised it.

He deepened the kiss, sliding his hand down the silky length of her nightgown to palm her breast, swallowing her gasp with his mouth. Her body yielded to his, her curves melting into his own hard planes as they kissed and kissed and still Alekos felt as if he could never get enough. He moved his hand from her breast to her hip, tugging the material upwards, needing to feel her skin against his. And when he did it only enflamed him more; the press of her naked hips and thighs against his made him arch into her, insistent need drumming through his body and drowning out thought.

'Alekos.' Iolanthe tore her mouth from his with a ragged grasp, slipping out of his arms so that in one instant it felt as if the heavens had opened and in the next he was left in the cold and the dark. 'We...we can't,' she gasped out, pulling her nightdress down. Alekos leaned against the wall, his heart thundering in his chest, blood beating loud in his ears. He could see plainly that Iolanthe was as affected as he was—her face was flushed, her lips swollen from his kisses, her eyes bright with the desire that had ignited between them in a scorching rush.

'You can't deny you want this,' he said.

'I don't deny it,' she admitted. 'How can I? But that doesn't mean it's the right time or place. Or...' she bit her lip, her gaze roving over him with undisguised hunger '...that it should happen at all.'

Alekos let out a huff of disbelieving laughter. 'Iolanthe, I've never had this kind of connection with a woman before. The sexual chemistry we have is explosive.' He reached one hand out to her, aching to touch her creamy skin once more. 'Why deny it? Or ourselves?'

'Because sexual gratification is not the be-all and end-all,' Iolanthe answered with force. 'I know that very well, Alekos. I've certainly gone without it for long enough.'

Even though it was the last thing he wanted to know, he heard himself ask, 'You and Lukas…?'

Deeper colour flared in Iolanthe's face. 'We never had that kind of relationship.'

'Never?' Alekos stared at her incredulously before a silly smile spread across his face.

Iolanthe saw and read it accurately. 'You Neanderthal,' she said, but there was a wry note of humour in her voice. 'Lukas wasn't… He didn't want me that way.'

'The man clearly was insane.'

'He was simply focused,' Iolanthe answered. 'And in any case, I never wanted him that way either. I suppose it pleases you to know you have been my only lover.'

'It humbles me,' Alekos admitted. 'But yes, it also thrills me. I don't want anyone else to experience with you what I have.'

'And if I demanded the same thing?' Iolanthe challenged.

'I haven't,' Alekos told her. 'Yes, I admit, in ten years there have been other women. But not many, certainly not as many as I can see you're thinking.'

'I wouldn't have expected anything else,' Iolanthe answered. 'We were finished before we began, Alekos.'

'But we're beginning again now,' Alekos said, the inflexible iron of determination in his voice. 'We've spent too much time staring backwards, Iolanthe. I want to look towards the future. I want to build that future with you.' He nodded towards the small space between them. 'I won't push you when it comes to this. But I won't pretend either. I want you in my bed. I want the taste of you on my lips and the feel of you on my hands. And most of all I want to move inside you as I once did—that moment has stayed with me all these years, Iolanthe. I've never felt with anyone else even a fraction of what I've felt with you, and I want to feel it again. Soon and often and very much.'

She stared at him with wide eyes, her tongue darting out to touch her lips, making him stifle a groan. 'That's... very clear.'

'Good,' Alekos answered, his gaze not leaving hers. 'Because I definitely don't want any doubts on that score.'

The next morning dawned bright and hot and Iolanthe lay in bed, enjoying the sun streaming through the windows as her body tingled from the memory of Alekos's kiss the night before. And the things he'd said...his words had held as much power as his touch.

Was it simply because she'd been starved of masculine affection for so long? Alekos's clearly stated desire for her thrilled her to the core. *Soon and often and very much.* She might have pushed him away last night, but she felt as he did. She wanted him as much as he wanted her.

Iolanthe rolled onto her stomach, hugging her pillow as she tried to ignore the flare of heat through her pelvis. Imagined Alekos touching her again, his hands knowing and caressing every dip and curve of her body, bringing her to heights of pleasure she'd only experienced once before.

From outside she heard the sound of splashing, and, grateful for a distraction from the hot ferment of her thoughts, she rose from her bed and threw open the shutters to the view of the pool and gardens, the sea twinkling in the distance.

Niko and Alekos were both in the pool, she saw with a dart of surprised pleasure. It was so unlike Niko to engage with anyone, especially someone he didn't really know. Maybe this was a sign of good things to come.

Iolanthe leaned her elbows on the windowsill and watched them for a moment; Niko stood at the edge of the pool, the water lapping his feet. Alekos had thrown a couple of inflatable pool toys into the water and was sitting at the edge, his hands braced behind him, his chest on glorious view.

Last night she'd only glimpsed those hard planes in the moonlit darkness, but now sunlight gilded his form, so he looked as if he'd been touched by the hand of heaven. He was stunningly fit, his chest and abs perfectly defined, the board shorts he wore slung low on his hips emphasising his powerful thighs.

Iolanthe sagged against the window, heat flaring again, hotter and more demanding than before. How could she resist him? *Why should she?*

Maybe sex could be the base from which they developed a trusting relationship. Except that hadn't worked out so well last time. As a naïve twenty-year-old she'd thought sex with Alekos meant they'd shared a connection. She'd been proved disastrously wrong, and she definitely didn't want to make that mistake again...no matter how tempted she was.

And Alekos wasn't offering anything *but* sex, she reminded herself. Not love or honesty or emotional intimacy. Whenever he'd talked about his childhood or anything important, he'd been reluctant, closed off. Did she really want to share the bed of a man whose heart was so clearly off limits?

'Hey.' Iolanthe blinked, startled from her thoughts, and saw Alekos smiling up at her. 'Why don't you come down and join us?'

A thrill of wary pleasure ran through her at the thought of them all spending time together. Like a family. 'Okay,' she said, and hurried to get her swimming costume.

A few minutes later she came down to the terrace, feeling shy in her modest tankini, aware of how much of her body was on display. Alekos didn't spare her blushes, letting his heated gaze linger on her breasts and thighs, a small smile curving his mouth.

'I like seeing you in a swimsuit,' he said, low enough so Niko, splashing in the other end of the pool, couldn't hear. 'I'd like you in a bikini even better.'

'You might not like the stretch marks so much,' Iolanthe returned with a little laugh of embarrassment. Her post-baby body wasn't quite as young and lithe as her twenty-year-old one had been.

'Stretch marks can be sexy,' Alekos told her, and now his grin was wicked. 'Especially when I know they were created by carrying my child.' With Niko looking the other way, he rested a hand possessively on her middle, fingers splayed. 'Almost as sexy as the thought of your stomach round with another child of mine.'

'Alekos.' Both scandalised and surprisingly turned on, Iolanthe jerked away. 'Really...'

'I'm not going to pretend I don't feel anything,' Alekos answered. 'Isn't that part of getting to know one another?'

'Yes...' Discomfited, Iolanthe spent an overlong time arranging her towel on one of the deck chairs. The trouble was, she didn't know what Alekos felt. He desired her, yes, she certainly got that. And he wanted to be involved in Niko's life, which she could certainly understand based on his own childhood. But his feelings for her? They still barely knew each other. Even as part of her wanted to plunge ahead recklessly and go with what Alekos was offering, another larger, saner part held back. Stayed safe. And tried desperately to keep from getting hurt again.

CHAPTER TWELVE

A WEEK PASSED in a lovely blur of sunny days. They spent a good deal of time lounging around the pool, and Niko's wary silences slowly melted into a timid and cautious friendliness. He still spent a good deal of his time alone, and getting him to talk could be hard work, but Iolanthe could see how her son was beginning to bloom, and it filled her with a fragile, hopeful joy.

Getting to know Alekos filled her with the same kind of joy. Over the last week he'd been patient, considerate, engaging, and interested in her. Iolanthe wasn't used to someone listening to her as if he really cared about what she said, or being solicitous about little things, whether it was pulling out her chair for her or fetching her a drink, asking her questions and wanting to hear the answer.

He had a surprising sense of humour too, self-deprecating and wry. She'd laughed more in the last week than she had in a long, long time.

And then of course there were the kisses. True to his word, Alekos hadn't pushed her for more, but he kissed her at every opportunity he got. Long, lingering kisses in the shadows or against a wall, and shorter ones in broad daylight, on the beach or the terrace. Kisses that made her whole body hum. She felt like the teenager she'd never been able to be, sneaking kisses, grinning guiltily. Feeling happy and free.

After a week on the island Alekos presented her with a sketchpad, a box of charcoal pencils, and a host of other art supplies. Iolanthe stared at them in delighted disbelief.

'Where did you...?'

'From Naxos. There's a little art shop there.'

She reached for an oil pastel, touching its silky tip with her thumb. 'You must have bought out the entire shop.'

'Just about.' Alekos smiled easily. 'I want you to enjoy yourself, rediscover your passions.' His eyes sparkled with both humour and something more as he added, 'All of them.'

'I'll start with drawing,' Iolanthe answered primly, but she was laughing, lit up inside. It felt dangerous to be this happy. To hope this much. She'd been so happy with Alekos this last week, but even amidst all the wonderful moments she'd seen how guarded he could be when she asked personal questions. He'd been happy for her to talk about herself, but he gave very little back. And she wondered if she just needed to be patient, or if she was chasing the end of the rainbow, never to be found.

Not wanting to dwell on such thoughts, she spent the morning sketching on the beach, Niko and Alekos playing together in the sea. She liked seeing Niko starting to hope, just as she was…and yet what if this all blew up in their faces? What if letting Alekos into their lives hurt them both, and this time worse than ever?

Alekos came out of the sea, water droplets beading on his burnished skin, making the doubts that had been circling Iolanthe's mind like crows fly away. She smiled at him, her gaze dropping to his chest, desire swirling in her veins.

'I like it when you look at me like that,' Alekos murmured as he stretched out on the sand next to her. 'I like it very much.'

Her cheeks heating, Iolanthe looked away to smile at Niko. 'Having fun?' she asked brightly and her son gave a small nod as he sat a little distance away from them, content to be on his own.

'Baby steps,' Alekos murmured. Iolanthe gave him a quick, grateful smile.

'I'm glad you're so patient.'

'I learned to be patient a long time ago.'

Curious, she asked, 'How so?'

Alekos's mouth tightened and something flashed in his eyes that reminded Iolanthe of how he'd been a week ago. Ten years ago. Reminded her that a week on she still didn't really know this man. 'Alekos...?'

'It's not important,' he answered with a shake of his head, and then turned to smile at Niko. 'How would you feel about sailing today?'

Niko's face brightened. 'In the yacht again?'

'No, in a little sailboat. You can try the rudder yourself, Niko.'

They spent the afternoon sailing, enjoying sun and sea, and the small confines of the boat gave Iolanthe little chance to talk with Alekos—or to kiss. With each day she was working up her courage to tell him she wanted more from the physical side of their relationship than just kisses...even though such an admission terrified her.

It's also only been one week. Are you really ready to trust him?

And not just with her body, but with her heart. Giving one, Iolanthe knew, meant giving the other.

Tired out from his afternoon on the water, Niko had an early dinner before heading to bed. Iolanthe went up to tuck him in, sitting on the edge of his bed, wishing he wanted a hug. 'Are you happy here, Niko?' she asked and he looked at her cautiously.

'Yes...but we're leaving soon, aren't we?'

Surprised, she drew back. 'Do you want to leave?'

Niko shrugged. 'We can't stay here for ever.'

No, they couldn't, but real life held little appeal. When she returned to Athens, Iolanthe knew she'd have to deal with all the pressing problems she'd left behind...like the state of Lukas's, and now her, finances.

Marriage to Alekos would solve that.

But that was the last reason why she should marry him,

or anyone. 'Do you like Alekos?' she asked Niko, and was rewarded with a distrustful glance.

'He's okay.'

'He likes you, you know.' Niko shrugged. 'Why don't you show him the apps you made? I think Alekos would really like to see them.' She knew he would, but convincing Niko that anything he did was interesting to someone else could be so hard.

Niko shook his head, the movement a gut reaction. 'No.'

'Niko...' Iolanthe sighed, knowing better than to press. 'Just because...because Lukas didn't like them doesn't mean Alekos wouldn't.'

Niko's eyes narrowed. 'Why did you call him Lukas?'

As opposed to Father. Iolanthe bit her lip. Everything felt complicated, a minefield of relationships. 'I don't know. I'm just saying, it might be worth a try.'

'I don't want to.' A refrain she felt she'd heard far too often. Niko snuggled down under the covers so only his golden-brown eyes were visible above the sheet. 'What if he didn't like them?' he asked in a voice so small Iolanthe struggled to hear it.

'Oh, Niko.' Her heart flooded with both love and sorrow. 'I know he will.'

'You can't know that,' Niko said. 'Not for certain.'

'No, but...' Iolanthe hesitated. Somehow in the last glorious week she and Alekos hadn't talked about when to tell Niko who he was. It seemed important now. 'I know he'd love to hear you talk about them,' she said. 'He's very proud of you.'

'Proud of me?' Disbelief and scorn twisted Niko's voice. 'He doesn't even know me. Who is he, anyway? Why are we even here?' He burrowed deeper beneath the covers and Iolanthe felt a frisson of fear. Niko's questions made sense, and she knew she and Alekos needed to talk about the future more than ever.

But what if she wasn't ready to talk about the future?

She wanted to stay on this island, enjoying paradise and forgetting there *was* a future.

'We're here to relax and enjoy ourselves,' she said carefully. 'And because Alekos is a friend. A...very good friend.'

Niko eyed her suspiciously from beneath the cover. 'How come I'd never met him before?'

Iolanthe stared at him helplessly. Each question he asked felt like a snare. Soon she would be completely tangled. 'There wasn't the opportunity, Niko. But you do... You do like Alekos, don't you?'

Her son's mouth settled into the frown. 'I told you, he's okay.'

'High praise indeed, then,' Iolanthe murmured wryly. She pressed his shoulder briefly in what passed for a good-night hug. She knew he wouldn't accept anything more. 'You should get some sleep, *pethi mou*. I'll see you in the morning.'

Downstairs the villa was quiet and peaceful, the first stars coming out in the sky. Iolanthe took a deep breath and let it out slowly, enjoying the stillness of the moment, the gentle swooshing sound of the waves on the beach and the distant clink of crystal from the terrace, where Alekos was pouring their evening drinks.

Over the last week they'd fallen into a pleasant routine of sharing a cocktail or aperitif on the terrace, either after dinner with Niko or before a meal they shared between just the two of them.

Now Iolanthe paused in the French windows and watched Alekos; she was half hidden by the gauzy curtains and could view him unobserved. He was as beautiful as ever, his hair black and damp from a shower after their afternoon of sailing, having exchanged his board shorts and T-shirt for a crisp white shirt and grey trousers. The sight of him made him catch her breath as she battled a wave of longing. The last week had gone a long way in helping her to trust, but she wasn't there yet. Sometimes she wondered if she ever would be, never mind the pulse-pounding lust she felt whenever she was near him.

He must have sensed her presence for he turned towards her, eyes narrowed against the glare of lights from the house, and Iolanthe stepped through the windows.

'I just settled Niko.'

Alekos handed her a glass of *retsina*. 'Is he all right?'

'Yes…' Iolanthe took a sip of the wine. 'He's fine. He enjoyed the sailing today.'

Alekos frowned, his gaze locked on hers over the rim of his glass. 'You don't sound completely sure.'

'He asked some things,' Iolanthe said after a moment. 'About you and who you are to us.'

Alekos stilled, his long, tapered fingers tensing on the crystal. 'And what did you say?'

'I said you were a friend. A very good friend. But it made me realise that such an answer won't satisfy him for very long.'

Iolanthe heard the pride in his voice as he answered, 'He's a bright, inquisitive boy.' He lowered his glass, his gaze seeming to burn into hers. 'And you know what solution I would suggest to this dilemma, Iolanthe.'

Her stomach somersaulted and she took another sip of wine. 'Do I?'

'We marry. As soon as possible.' Alekos didn't look away as he continued, iron entering his tone, 'I've been patient.'

'Alekos, it's been a *week*.' Iolanthe drew a shuddering breath, torn between temptation and sanity, or at least self-protection. 'That's not very long at all.'

'It's long in my book.'

'I suppose a week is a long time for you to cultivate a relationship,' she retorted, jealousy spiking hard, but Alekos shook his head, refusing to be deterred.

'There are no other women in my life now, and you've deprived me of my son for long enough.'

She drew back, stung. 'You still blame me—'

'I don't want to talk about the past,' Alekos dismissed, utterly implacable. 'It's no longer relevant.'

'Yet you just *said*—'

'I won't take no for an answer, Iolanthe. Not when it comes to Niko. Not when it comes to marriage.'

She took a deep breath, struggling to frame her response. 'I've been forced into one marriage already. I don't appreciate being forced into another.'

'And I don't appreciate being forced onto the sidelines,' Alekos returned with heat. 'What are you afraid of?' he demanded. 'A marriage between us is the obvious answer, and the chemistry is certainly there.' His eyes flashed with desire even now. 'Or would you like me to prove it to you?'

'No.' The word was a lie. 'But...I don't want another cold, loveless marriage, Alekos. I want more from my life than that.'

He stilled, his expression turning guarded. 'I thought... you said before you weren't interested in love.'

'I wasn't, not with Lukas.' Too late she realised how that sounded, and she saw the look of appalled surprise on Alekos's face. 'I mean... I don't want to be lonely. To be shut out of someone's life.'

Alekos's expression cleared. Clearly the thought of her falling in love with him had been anathema. Iolanthe didn't know whether to laugh or cry at how horrified he'd looked. 'You won't be.'

'What do you see a marriage between us actually looking like?' Iolanthe asked cautiously.

'Like this week,' Alekos answered. 'But better. Definitely better at night.'

She couldn't miss the sexual innuendo laced in his words, the heat in his gaze. 'What are you really afraid of, Iolanthe?' Alekos asked in a low voice. He took a step closer to her so she felt a dizzying wave of need crash over her, a reaction simply to his nearness.

'Lots of things,' she managed. 'So many...'

'Name them.' He stared at her in challenge, but there was also kindness in his eyes. Iolanthe took a deep breath. *Trust.* That was what this was about.

'I'm scared of Niko flipping out,' she said frankly. It was easier to start with their son's issues rather than her own fears.

'Why would he flip out? Because he's learned the truth, that the man who rejected him wasn't his father, and the man who is, who already loves and accepts him, is waiting, *wanting* to be acknowledged?' His voice throbbed with emotion and Iolanthe's mouth dropped open in startled amazement as tears stung her eyes.

'Do you mean that?' she whispered.

'I wouldn't have said it otherwise.'

'You...love Niko? I mean, now that you know him and not just because he's your son?'

Alekos hesitated, and Iolanthe saw the surprise in his eyes. He wasn't used to the idea of loving someone. And while he might love his son, he still didn't want to love her. 'Yes. I love him.' He sounded wondering, and it made her smile even as sorrow pierced her at how much they'd all missed out on. 'I know it's still early days, and we have a long way to go as a family, but I love him, Iolanthe. I want him in my life. I want you in my life.'

Iolanthe let out a choked laugh. 'You make it sound so simple.'

'Maybe it is.'

'You love Niko,' Iolanthe challenged, 'but you're not interested in any other love? In loving me?' The words sounded needy but she knew she had to have the answer to her question.

Alekos drew back, a veil dropping into place, hiding his emotions. 'Why are you asking me that?'

'I'm just trying to understand.'

'I don't want this to be more complicated than it has to be,' Alekos answered carefully. 'A love between a parent and child, a father and son—that's simple. A biological fact.'

'And between a man and a woman?' Iolanthe asked shakily.

'I'm not sure where you're going with this,' he said after a charged pause, his voice toneless. 'Or what you want me to say.'

'I don't know,' Iolanthe admitted on a wild laugh that ended with a sad sigh. 'I realise I'm just stating the obvious.' She took a deep breath, trying to marshal her thoughts and keep a sudden, surprising disappointment at bay.

'Iolanthe,' Alekos asked in a low voice. 'What is it?'

'I just feel...sad,' she said after a pause. She turned to look at him, her expression open and, she feared, far too revealing. 'I survived ten years of a loveless marriage, Alekos, and it nearly sucked the soul out of me. I don't want another like it.'

'I told you, ours wouldn't be like that,' he answered, heat in his voice.

'And yet you're still not interested in love,' Iolanthe stated. 'Not in loving *me*, anyway.' She searched his face, saw the answer in the shuttering of his eyes, the tightening of his jaw. 'No matter what you said about wanting me,' she finished. 'Or me being the only woman in your life.'

'I'm not sure what love has to do with it,' Alekos said. His voice had gone toneless again, as if he was erasing emotion from his voice, his heart. If there had been any there to begin with. 'I asked you in the beginning,' he continued, 'and you said it wasn't something you wanted. Did you lie to me about that?'

'I didn't *lie*,' Iolanthe answered hotly. She felt shaken both by Alekos's sudden coolness and the realisation that was pounding through her. A week of fun and sun and kisses had woken up her long-dormant heart with all of its unreasonable longings. A week ago, before coming here, she hadn't dared to dream of love. She'd put away all of her young hopes into a box and locked them deep inside her. Coming here, spending time with Alekos, had sent them hurtling out. Too bad Alekos wasn't interested in those.

'So?' Alekos prompted, a muscle flexing in his jaw. 'What has changed?'

'Nothing, I just...' Iolanthe stared at him helplessly, unwilling to explain how *she'd* changed. How she might already be falling in love with him. Alekos wasn't interested in that; he'd made it perfectly clear. He wanted her in his bed and he wanted to be involved in Niko's life. That was what marriage was about, no matter what promises he made about never hurting her. 'I'm just processing all of this,' she said at last. 'And what it means. Marriage is a big step, Alekos. You seem to think it's simple.'

'It seems a simple decision to make, considering what's involved,' Alekos answered tersely. He blew out a breath. 'But I understand your reservations, Iolanthe. Even if I seem impatient. It's only...' A smile curved his mouth as he plucked the half-drunk glass of *retsina* from her hand and tossed it down onto a table. 'I want you so much.'

Want, not love. It was something, she supposed. Alekos slid his arms around her waist and drew her close as Iolanthe tilted her head up for a kiss, craving his touch even now. Especially now. Alekos desired her. Maybe, just maybe, she could let that be enough.

CHAPTER THIRTEEN

ALEKOS WATCHED IOLANTHE and Niko chat over his laptop and tried to ignore the savage twisting in his gut that last night's conversation—and unsated lust—had caused. What had Iolanthe been going on about, talking about love? He'd thought they were on the same page. He'd expected her to want what he did...a marriage of expediency and desire.

Except, he acknowledged with a twinge of unease, somehow in the last week what he'd wanted had started to change. He liked spending time with Iolanthe, talking to her and, yes, kissing her. Hell, yes. But that wasn't *love*. That wasn't needing a person to complete you, to make you happy. He never wanted to feel that way again. He knew where it led. He'd loved both his mother and father that way and they'd left him without so much as a backward glance. The ensuing years hadn't shown him any different, and he wasn't about to give Iolanthe the opportunity to do the same. He wasn't going to give her his heart.

His body, yes. His friendship. His devotion, even, and his unwavering loyalty. But the heart of him, the tender, fragile, vulnerable organ that he'd sealed in steel and cold-blooded ambition and revenge—that wasn't up for discussion. At all.

'Alekos?' Iolanthe turned a smiling glance on him, and he was glad to see how relaxed she seemed, considering how close they'd come to an argument last night. 'Niko wants to show you something.'

'Okay.' He rose from his deck chair and went to join them at the table on the terrace. Niko was ducking his head, refusing to meet his eye, and Alekos waited, understanding and accepting now that his son needed time.

'Show him, Niko,' Iolanthe urged. 'Alekos will be so pleased.'

'I'm sure I will,' Alekos added, even though he had no idea what Niko intended to show him. After a few endless seconds the boy wordlessly pushed the laptop over so Alekos could see the screen. Confused, Alekos looked at Niko, but his head was lowered, his fringe covered his face so he couldn't tell what his son was thinking. He looked at the computer screen instead.

It took him a few seconds to realise he was seeing the complicated coding for a mobile app. Quite complicated, he realised, and he glanced sharply at Niko. 'Did you do this?'

Niko flinched and shrunk back. 'Yes...' he muttered.

'By yourself?'

'Yes...'

Alekos glanced at the coding again. 'Niko, that's remarkable. A boy your age...' He shook his head, impressed and also excited. 'Show me the app.'

A shy, incredulous smile dawning across his face, Niko leaned forward and pressed a few buttons. Alekos watched, transfixed, grasping the gist of it quickly. 'So these power points...the app keeps track of them on your phone and alerts you...'

Niko nodded eagerly, and Iolanthe laughed. 'I think I'll leave you two to your zombies,' she said lightly, and squeezed Alekos's shoulder as she passed. He gave her a quick smile before turning back to the laptop, both of them engrossed in what was on the screen.

Iolanthe felt as if her heart was full to overflowing with thankfulness. Alekos *got* it. He got Niko; he understood and was excited by what her—*their*—son was doing. It was more than she'd ever hoped for, more than she'd dared to dream.

And for a few seconds it filled her with regret for what could have been, if Alekos had been more forgiving ten years ago, if she'd had more courage.

But no more regrets. Iolanthe had had enough of those. She wanted to think of the future now, and what it could hold for her, Niko, and Alekos. She'd had a lot to think about these last few days, a lot of things to weigh up in the balance and decide if they equalled out. If what Alekos was offering was enough. And she was starting to believe that maybe, just maybe, it could be.

An hour later Alekos came and found Iolanthe sitting on the beach, her legs stretched out in front of her and her hands braced behind, the sea breeze whipping her hair into dark tangles around her face.

'Sorry that took so long,' he said as he sat down next to her.

'I'm happy you had the time with Niko. You saw all his apps?'

'Yes, they're brilliant.' Alekos shook his head in wonder, pride evident in his voice and face. 'Really brilliant. I wish he'd shown them to me before.'

'He showed them to Lukas,' Iolanthe said quietly. 'He... he wasn't interested.'

Alekos's face darkened briefly before he set his jaw. 'That's in the past. Things are different now. I'm going to market Niko's apps through my company, with his help.'

'He'll love that, but...' Iolanthe hesitated, not wanting to ruin the happy moment and yet feeling it too deeply not to say something. 'What about Petra Innovation, Alekos?'

Alekos's expression didn't change but she felt a tension run through his body. 'What about it?'

'You know it means a lot to Niko—and to me. My father built the company from nothing—'

Alekos let out a bark of ugly laughter. 'From nothing?'

Iolanthe drew back, stung by his tone. His whole attitude. 'Is this about what happened years ago?' she asked. 'About some design my father had that you didn't?' She'd pushed that knowledge to the back of her mind, not wanting it to pollute what she and Alekos were trying to build. Whatever happened had been years ago. She'd wanted to believe they could move on from that.

Alekos squinted out at the sea. 'Let's leave the past in the past, Iolanthe. Niko is my son. His inheritance is Demetriou Tech.' When he turned to face her his expression was final and closed. 'Let's leave it at that.'

'And Petra Innovation—'

'I'm not willing to discuss it.' Iron had entered his tone, leaving Iolanthe frustrated and silent. She and Alekos had been getting along so well, and yet at times like this she wondered if it was all a mirage. A fantasy. When it came to something important, something that mattered to her, he refused to bend at all. And she couldn't help but feel he'd closed off a whole part of himself that he would never let her get to know.

But maybe instead of backing off, shying away, Iolanthe thought with a tremor of fear, she needed to go forward. She needed to dare. How else could she and Alekos move past this? One of them had to take a chance. A leap into the unknown, no matter how scary it was.

The questions pinged through her mind and sent up a swarm of butterflies in her stomach. *What was she really thinking of?*

'Okay, Alekos,' she said quietly. 'We'll leave it at that.' For now.

Twilight was settling on the sea as Alekos stared unseeingly out of his bedroom window. The conversation he'd had with Iolanthe that afternoon had left him restless, caught between a desire to forget everything that had gone before and knowing with unswerving uncertainty that he couldn't. Damn Talos Petrakis and his unending legacy of betrayal and revenge. How could he explain to Iolanthe what her father had done? She might not even believe him, and if she did the knowledge of her father's actions would hurt her unbearably.

Why couldn't she just leave it? Why did she have to care so much about her father's wretched company? Uttering a groan, Alekos turned from the window. He and Iolanthe had called a truce for the rest of the day, or so he'd hoped. They'd kept conversation deliberately light and had had a family dinner with Niko. Alekos had eschewed their nightly ritual of drinks out on the terrace while Iolanthe put Niko to bed. And now he was here, alone, restless, uncertain, unsated.

A light knock sounded on the door. Alekos tensed.

'Yes?'

'Alekos?' Iolanthe pushed open the door, standing hesitantly on the threshold.

'What are you doing here?' She blinked at his harsh tone, and inwardly he cursed. He hadn't meant to sound unwelcoming, but he'd been so surprised to see her. 'I'm glad to see you, of course,' he added quickly. 'Come in.'

She stepped into the room, closing the door behind her. She'd changed from her shorts and T-shirt of earlier to a shift dress in pale lavender that showed her newly golden tan to effect, and her hair was tousled about her shoulders. Despite her air of uncertainty, a look of intent gleamed in her eyes.

'You didn't come down to the terrace.'

'I thought you were putting Niko to bed.'

She cocked her head, her gaze sweeping over him. 'Did you want to be left alone?'

'No,' he said, his voice slightly hoarse. Iolanthe had started to walk towards him, hips subtly swaying, a hesitant smile curving her mouth. 'I thought you did.'

'I don't.'

'Okay, then.'

Iolanthe stood before him, that small, strange smile still curving her lips, a pulse beating wildly at her throat. She was close enough that he could inhale the scent of her, sunshine and vanilla and warm woman. Alekos swallowed, aware of how his heart had started to thud in response.

Iolanthe lifted her hand and placed it on his cheek, as he'd once done to her a lifetime ago. She trailed her fingers along his cheek until her thumb rested on the pad of his lower lip, just as he'd done. Now the seducer had become the seduced. 'Alekos...' she began, and then hesitated. He could see the nervousness in her eyes, hear it in her voice. 'I'm ready,' she whispered.

Alekos's heart slammed against his ribcage. 'Ready...'

She took a step closer so her dress brushed his legs and her breasts nudged his chest. 'I hope you know what I mean,' she said, and then let out a throaty laugh that nearly sent Alekos to his knees.

'I know.' Yet this was the last thing he'd expected tonight. He'd been up here angsting about their future when Iolanthe had intended to seduce him. Alekos didn't know whether to laugh or to groan.

'Well...' She lifted her eyebrows, clearly expecting him to take over. And Alekos almost did, because that would be so easy. So wonderful. Hadn't he been waiting for this? Longing for them both to put the past behind them? But something made him hesitate, and then he lifted his eyebrows right back at her.

'Well?'

'I thought...' She nibbled her lip, uncertainty chasing her earlier confidence across her face.

Alekos hooked his thumbs in his belt loops and gave her a small, teasing smile. 'I thought you were calling the shots here.'

Her eyes widened in shock. 'But...'

'But what?' Alekos flung his arms wide, enjoying the

moment more than he'd ever expected to. 'Seduce me, Iolanthe.'

She laughed softly. 'Alekos, I've had one sexual experience in my life and that was ten years ago. You really think I can seduce you?'

She spoke lightly enough, but Alekos saw the doubt in her eyes and knew his gut instinct had been right. Iolanthe needed this. She needed to believe in herself as a sexually confident woman, in them as a couple that could still burn up the sheets. He had no doubts about either.

Smiling, he reached for her hand and laced his fingers through hers, drawing her even closer so their bodies were pressed together. 'Iolanthe,' he murmured, 'that one sexual experience marked me for life. I've never forgotten it. Never equalled it. *Seduce* me, woman.'

She laughed again, a soft huff of sound, and then, with a flash of challenge and courage lighting her eyes, she went on her tiptoes and brushed her mouth against his. 'If you insist,' she whispered.

Alekos could tell she was still waiting for him to take the lead, and it was an effort not to. Everything in him was roaring to pull her into his arms and devour her with his kiss. He resisted, though, and stood still instead, his lips parting under hers in silent encouragement.

She tilted her head back, her gaze moving over his face. 'Alekos…?'

'I know you can do better than that.'

Alarm flashed in her eyes but then was swiftly gone, and a small, sensual smile tugged at her mouth. 'Maybe I can,' she said, and kissed him again.

Iolanthe hadn't expected this. In truth she hadn't pictured anything beyond opening Alekos's bedroom door besides a few hazy and very pleasant images, but for Alekos to surrender control? To ask her to take the lead?

To *seduce* him?

The prospect, she realised with a ripple of shock, was completely thrilling. Ten long years of letting the sexual side of her fade away, suppressing natural desire and hopeless yearning, now created in her a maelstrom of want. And she could give into it. She could decide what happened, when, how much. And she wanted *much*.

'I didn't think you liked giving up control,' she teased.

'On occasion, when it's warranted.'

She laughed softly. 'That sounds like you.' She hesitated, wondering how to begin. How did you seduce a man, and especially a man like Alekos? Powerful, sexual, charismatic, and undeniably attractive?

'I'm waiting,' Alekos teased softly.

'Right.' Two butterfly kisses and Alekos was still waiting, an expectant look on his face, a small smile quirking his mouth. Iolanthe decided she needed to up her game.

'So this,' she said as she tugged at his T-shirt. 'This can go.'

'All right.' Obediently Alekos raised his hands above his head and Iolanthe stood on her tiptoes to tug his shirt off, leaving his chest bare.

She'd seen his chest bare a lot over the last week, when they'd been swimming and sailing. But she hadn't touched it. She hadn't let her hands slide over the silky, hair-roughened skin, flexing on the perfectly sculpted pectoral muscles, dipping lower to the six-pack abs that tensed under her questing fingers.

Alekos's breath came out in a low hiss. 'You're doing pretty well so far.'

She shot him a wicked smile, buoyed by confidence, by *power*. 'I've barely started.'

'That,' Alekos told her in a near-growl, 'is a relief.'

Except despite her big talk, Iolanthe realised she wasn't actually sure how to go on. On that lovely, lost night ten years ago Alekos had taken complete control. All she'd had to do was say yes.

She danced her fingers up his torso simply to give her time to think. To dare. And she enjoyed the feel of him, the way his muscles flexed in response to her every touch.

'You're torturing me, you know,' Alekos said in a ragged voice, and Iolanthe's hands stilled.

'Am I?' she asked, uncertain and a little alarmed, and then a sudden, entirely feminine surge of power went through her and she slid her hands down to the waistband of his trousers. 'Is that a bad thing?' she asked and basked in the tawny glow of Alekos's eyes.

Her fingers trembled only a little as she undid his belt buckle and slid it from its loops, and then popped the button on his trousers and tugged down the zip, her insides lurching with desire and a little trepidation at the hard length of him.

Alekos kicked off his trousers and then nodded towards her. 'I'm not the only one stripping down, am I?'

'No...' She reached back for the zip but in her flustered state she couldn't get it and wordlessly Alekos turned her around and then in one fluid movement unzipped her dress.

The shift fell away and with a simple shrug of her shoulders it came down to her waist. She felt Alekos's fingers on her back, cool and sure, unsnapping her bra.

'I thought I was the one calling the shots.'

'Just helping things along,' Alekos murmured as he pressed a kiss to the nape of her neck. 'Otherwise I might explode.'

Iolanthe shuddered under his touch, leaning into him, sighing with pleasure as he brought his hands around to cup her breasts and get rid of the flimsy scrap of lace that had been covering them.

'I've dreamed of this,' he murmured as his thumbs flicked over the aching peaks and his hips nudged her bottom meaningfully. 'Dreamed and dreamed.'

'I have too,' Iolanthe whispered. A thrill went through

her every time Alekos moved against her, and suddenly she wasn't sure she could draw out this erotic foreplay any longer. Her need was too great.

She turned around in his arms, pressing against him as she wrapped her arms around his neck and brought his lips down to hers. 'Kiss me, Alekos. Kiss me like you mean it.' Because even if she didn't have his love, she needed that assurance. Desperately.

And he did kiss her, his mouth devouring hers, his tongue sweeping inside and claiming her so she felt that kiss right down to her toenails.

Still it wasn't enough. Alekos steered her towards the bed, cushioning her fall onto the mattress with his arm as he kept kissing her, his mouth not leaving hers as she lay down on the bed and he stretched out on top of her.

The feel of his legs against hers, the thrust of his arousal against her belly, his hard chest pressing her deeper into the mattress...it was all exquisite, overwhelming, and yet still not enough.

Her legs tangled with his as she arched upwards, seeking more. Needing more.

When he slid his hand between her thighs she cried out; it had been so long since she'd felt a man's intimate touch. It had been a lifetime; she'd lived and died and was now coming to life again under his hands.

'Alekos...' She let out a sob of frustration as he withdrew his hand, needing him to touch her more and deeper still, but then he was poised above her and finally, *finally* he was sliding inside, the sweet invasion everything she'd ever wanted, the answer to the questions she'd been asking for far too long.

'Is this all right?' Alekos asked, and Iolanthe nodded frantically.

'Yes...*yes*...' It felt strange and stretching and definitely wonderful. Her body opened to accommodate him, and then he began to move, and Iolanthe gave herself up to the pounding rhythm and the crashing waves of sensation, until with a cry she collapsed into him, arms and legs wrapping around him, drawing him tighter to herself as colours and lights danced before her eyes and her body pulsed with the pleasure it had been so long denied.

Alekos sagged against her with his own deep sigh of satisfaction, and then he braced himself on one arm, easing back so he could brush a tendril of hair from her cheek and kiss her on the lips with aching gentleness.

The words *I love you* hovered in the air between them so Iolanthe wasn't sure if she'd said them or Alekos had. Then she realised that of course no one had, they were just in her head, in her throat, bursting to get out.

Before coming into Alekos's bedroom she'd given herself a stern talking-to, insisting she wasn't going to go looking for love. She was going to be satisfied, be happy with what Alekos was offering her. What they already had. Seemed as if her heart hadn't got the memo.

Mercifully, as Alekos rolled away from her, she swallowed the words down. No point in saying them. Not now, not ever. This was what she had chosen, the kind of life she could look forward to. It was more than she'd ever had before. She'd told herself it could be enough.

Alekos lay there for a few minutes, one arm flung over his head, uncomfortably reminding Iolanthe of how things had ended ten years ago. Two sexual experiences in her entire life and they were starting to feel terrifyingly similar. She felt just as uncertain and exposed now as she did then, and she didn't like it one bit.

Then Alekos lowered his arm and smiled at her. 'That was amazing.'

Relief pulsed through her, along with a treacherous little flicker of disappointment. She would have preferred *I love you*. By a long shot. But she'd take amazing, she told herself. She'd have to.

'Yes, it was, wasn't it?' she agreed with a teasing smile.

She could do light. She might feel a million things far too strongly, but she knew how to put a happy face on when required. And she *was* happy. It *had* been amazing.

Alekos rose from the bed and reached for his boxers, his back to her. Clearly moving on, then. Iolanthe felt she had no choice but to cover up as well.

She grabbed her dress from the floor and was about to wriggle into it when Alekos turned around, stilling at the sight of her, a frown creasing his forehead.

'Wait.'

'What?' She clutched the dress to her chest and tried not to blush.

'I didn't mean...' He raked a hand through his hair. 'You don't need to get dressed. I don't want you to leave.'

'You...don't?'

'I want you in my bed,' Alekos answered. He pulled back the duvet and slipped back into bed beside her before taking her into his arms. 'I want you in my bed all night, preferably.'

Even as Iolanthe thrilled to the words, she hesitated. 'Niko...'

'I know.' Alekos tightened his embrace, tucking her head into his shoulder. She breathed in the warm male scent of him and felt herself start to relax. 'You can go back to your room before morning. Just...stay with me for now.' The request sounded strange, hesitant, as if it was more than he was comfortable admitting. And it made Iolanthe ache.

'Okay,' she whispered as she snuggled into him. 'I'll stay.' For as long as he wanted.

CHAPTER FOURTEEN

'I NEED TO return to Athens.'

Iolanthe tried not to let her face fall as her heart was doing at Alekos's simple statement. Of course he needed to go back to Athens. He was an important and successful man of business, and he had work to do. So did she, for that matter. She needed to deal with Lukas's estate, get Niko back to his lessons, and basically sort her whole life out. Their two-week island idyll was over, even if she didn't want it to be.

'When?' she asked, struggling to keep her tone light and interested, as if this were no big deal. As if she weren't apprehensive—no, *terrified*—about what the future looked like for her, for Niko, for them as a family. As a couple. For the last week, since she'd first shared Alekos's bed, she felt as if she'd been living in a dream. Days spent with Niko and Alekos, swimming, playing, and even some drawing. She had a whole notebook of island sketches she wanted to continue to work on.

And the nights had been spent with Alekos. Over the last week they'd explored each other's bodies and given each other more pleasure than Iolanthe, in her earlier innocence, could have ever imagined.

But it was easy on a private island, with no other distractions or temptations, to indulge each other. To start relaxing and feeling as if this were real life.

What would happen when they got back to Athens?

'We should leave tomorrow,' Alekos said. 'I've left things too long as it is.'

'Tomorrow...' Iolanthe gazed out at the shimmering sea, the sun just starting its descent. They were sitting on the terrace, sipping iced tea while Niko had one last swim in the pool. Her body felt pleasantly relaxed and tired from a day of sailing—and a night of lovemaking. The thought of getting back on the yacht, returning to Athens, made her insides tighten with tension and anxiety. Alekos might not love her, but he'd given more and more of himself while on this island. What if he yanked it all back, once they returned to Athens?

'I should have said something earlier,' Alekos said. 'We could have prepared Niko. I just didn't want to think about it.'

'I understand.' Iolanthe gave him a fleeting smile. 'I feel the same.'

'I have to go to New York City next week,' Alekos said abruptly. 'And I'd like you to go with me.'

New York. Just as she'd always wanted to, stroll through Greenwich Village and sketch in Central Park. Even so Iolanthe remained guarded. 'Niko has lessons, Alekos. And I'm not sure letting him traipse around the globe—'

'I wasn't talking about Niko. Just you.'

Her breath came out in a shocked rush. 'What…?'

Alekos leaned forward. 'Iolanthe, have you ever been without Niko? He has his lessons at home, you rarely go out, and your whole life has been wrapped up in him—'

'I want to be a good mother,' Iolanathe interjected, stung by his assessment. 'I would have thought you could understand that.'

'I do understand it,' Alekos answered. 'But it isn't healthy, how sequestered you've been. You need a life of your own, interests of your own. Time to yourself and time just for us.'

'We've had plenty of time just the two of us this week,' Iolanthe retorted.

'I don't mean just in the bedroom,' Alekos answered, heat flaring in his eyes just at the mention—and the memories. 'Time to spend together, as a couple.'

She let out a huff of laughter. 'I can't believe I'm getting relationship advice from you.'

His lips quirked in a rueful smile of acknowledgement. 'Perhaps you'll take it as a sign of how much I want this—us—to work.'

His words left her speechless. How could she resist or resent that? It was what she wanted too, even if she was scared to admit as much. Even if she was scared to hope, to dream. Yet he still wasn't promising to love her, she reminded herself. She'd been careful not to talk about anything that would make Alekos guarded over the last week. No deep emotion, no personal questions. As long as she walked that tightrope, everything was fine. But what happened when she slipped? When she fell off?

'What would I do with Niko?' she asked, mainly to stall for time.

'You have a housekeeper. Couldn't she keep an eye on him for a few days? Two nights.'

Two nights. Time alone with the man she was coming to love. And he wanted it with her. *Be happy with that, Iolanthe. Don't be greedy for more.* Iolanthe swallowed dryly. If she was trying to keep herself safe, she'd already failed, so maybe she should just go for it. Say yes. Live the dream...or as much as Alekos was offering her.

'Okay,' she whispered, and Alekos smiled in satisfaction.

A week later Iolanthe sat in first class, a flute of champagne clenched between her fingers as the plane took off into an azure sky.

The last week's re-entry into real life had been a little bumpy, but not nearly as bad as Iolanthe had feared. Niko had been disappointed to leave the island, and more guarded with Alekos now that they were no longer hidden away in paradise. Iolanthe had tried to talk to him about it, but Niko had been as reluctant as ever to share what he was feeling. In the end Iolanthe had decided to give him time to adjust, just as she needed.

She hadn't actually seen that much of Alekos as he'd been preoccupied with catching up with work, and she'd been busy settling back into normal life and also dealing with Lukas's estate. Just as she'd feared, there was very little money left outside her shares in Petra Innovation. Perhaps she should agree to dismantle the company, even though the prospect tore at her heart. And Alekos surely wouldn't destroy the company, now that he knew how important it was to Niko. He might have been reluctant to talk about it, but Iolanthe had to believe Alekos wouldn't act so callously towards his son.

She'd seen him twice over the course of the last week, and it had only taken a few days on her own to make her question every decision she'd made, every hope she'd dared to harbour.

Now Alekos leaned across her seat to squeeze her hand. 'Don't worry so much.'

'How do you know I'm worrying?'

'Your eyes glaze over with panic.' He gave her a small, teasing smile. 'You look like a rabbit seeing a snare. Niko will be all right, Iolanthe. This is a chance for him to have a little independence as much as it is for us.'

Iolanthe nodded, even though she was just as worried about them as she was about Niko. 'What work do you have in the States?' she asked, mainly to distract herself from the fears flitting through her mind and the nerves churning in her stomach.

'I'm partnering with a firm in America to launch a new software system.'

'Partnering?' Iolanthe repeated and then continued before she could think better of it. 'Couldn't you do that with Petra Innovation?'

Alekos's expression of smiling ease shut right down. 'Let's not talk about business.'

Which reminded her of something Lukas or her father would say. Gritting her teeth, Iolanthe looked out of the window. This was the kind of thing she was afraid of. Old habits died hard, and, no matter how teasing or flirtatious or kind Alekos could be, at his core was something Iolanthe could neither penetrate nor understand. A part of himself he didn't want her to understand—this burning drive, this closed mentality.

She knew better than to press the issue, and yet the whole conversation, or lack of it, made her realise she still didn't know what Alekos intended for her father's company. She'd comforted herself that he wouldn't shut it down, for Niko's sake, but now she realised he'd given her no cause to think that. And what kind of relationship did they even have if she felt she couldn't ask about it?

Knowing she had no answers now, she pushed the worries and questions out of her mind and determined to enjoy what could be an amazing few days, if she just let go of her worries.

Alekos watched with relief as the frown that had settled between Iolanthe's eyebrows gradually smoothed out. Two glasses of champagne helped, he supposed, and he'd worked hard to keep the mood upbeat and light. He didn't know what she worried about, whether it was Niko or something bigger. Something like *them*.

He had a diamond and emerald ring in his attaché that he intended to present to her tonight, while they had dinner at one of the city's most exclusive restaurants. He hoped a formal and romantic proposal might help put Iolanthe's lingering doubts to rest.

And as for his doubts? Alekos pushed those away with one decisive shove. He didn't like Iolanthe asking about his plans for Petra Innovation, but he told himself that in light of what they had together, both as a couple and as a family, her concerns about her father's company would pale.

Niko would have Demetriou Tech, which was an even bigger and better inheritance. Surely that would satisfy her.

As soon as they landed at JFK, Alekos whisked Iolanthe away in a stretch limo, enjoying the way she revelled in the luxury, laughing and shaking her head as he topped up her glass of champagne once again.

'I feel like a movie star,' she teased.

'That's how I want you to feel.'

'Is that how you feel?' For a moment Iolanthe dropped the banter. 'You know, you don't need to impress me, Alekos,' she said quietly. 'At least, not with this.' She raised her glass in an ironic toast that Alekos suspected encompassed everything—the limo, the luxury hotel he'd booked them into, his life. 'What impresses me,' she continued, 'is how patient you've been with both Niko and me. How thoughtful and considerate. That's what makes me—' she stopped abruptly, and Alekos tensed, his insides icing as he realised what she'd been going to say '—care about you,' she finished, and glanced away from him, out of the window. 'Is that the Empire State Building? Amazing.'

'No, it's the Harlem River Park Tower,' Alekos returned dryly. 'Trust me, the Empire State Building is much better.' Love, he realised hollowly. She'd been going to say love.

While Iolanthe continued to peer out of the window Alekos tried to untangle his reaction to Iolanthe's almost declaration. *Love.* He'd told her he had no interest in love. *She'd* said she had no interest in love, even when she'd pressed the point back on the island. When he'd envisioned their marriage, it had always been an arrangement of convenience—and pleasure. But love?

Had Iolanthe changed her mind about love? Had he changed his?

The thought of loving someone made Alekos's stomach clench in remembered shame and desperation. Begging his father not to go. Pleading with his mother to let him stay. And then Talos Petrakis... His stomach cramped harder.

He might not have *loved* Petrakis, but he'd seen him as a father figure. He'd trusted him, looked up to him, cared. He never wanted to feel that way again, hopeless, helpless, the victim of his own emotions—and others' scheming.

But what if loving Iolanthe didn't make him feel that way?

The question felt like a firework going off in his brain. Leaning back in his seat, Alekos drained his glass of champagne and chose not to answer it.

Fortunately they both recovered their equilibrium over the course of the drive into the city, and by the time they'd reached the penthouse suite of the hotel Alekos had booked, he felt his old, implacable self, happy to pull Iolanthe into his arms and kiss her thoroughly as he backed her towards the enormous king-sized bed, with floor-to-ceiling windows overlooking Central Park forty floors below.

'Time to christen the bedroom.'

She laughed and didn't resist as he tossed her gently onto the bed before joining her there.

'I did want to see the Empire State Building,' she murmured half-heartedly as Alekos expertly undid the zip on her dress.

'You can. Later.'

'And Greenwich Village...' Her words ended on a breathy sigh as Alekos peeled the dress from her body and bent his head to her breasts. 'We can do that later,' she agreed and reached for the buttons on his shirt.

'Definitely,' Alekos promised. They had more important things to do now.

Several hours later Iolanthe gazed out at the sparkling vista of the city skyline while Alekos finished dressing. Her body felt both tingly and tired from their lovemaking this afternoon; they never had made it to the Empire State Building. Iolanthe didn't think either of them minded.

She could be happy, she told herself, with what Alekos was offering her. How much—or, really, how little. So love wasn't on the table for him. She understood that, especially considering his difficult childhood. And she decided that perhaps she could live without love if she had all the other things Alekos was promising—trust, affection, loyalty, devotion. Really, what was love compared to that?

And so what if she still felt as if part of him, maybe even the most important part, was locked away from her and always would be? She had the rest of him, and that had to be enough. It was certainly more than she'd had in her last marriage.

'Enjoying the view?' Alekos came up behind her to rest his hands on her shoulders.

'Yes, it's amazing,' Iolanthe said, although for the last few minutes she'd been so lost in her thoughts none of it had registered. Alekos dropped a kiss on the back of her neck and Iolanthe shuddered in response before finding the strength to step away. 'I want to see some of this city before we go back to Greece,' she said lightly.

'And I want to show it to you,' Alekos answered. He took her by the hand and led her from the suite to their limo waiting downstairs, and Iolanthe determined to enjoy this evening and stop worrying about what she didn't have.

The restaurant Alekos took her to was as luxurious as everything else in his life, and their private table had floor-to-ceiling views of the city. The champagne had just been poured, their meals ordered, when Alekos, to Iolanthe's shock, dropped to one knee.

'What...?' she began dazedly, even though she knew what Alekos had to be doing. She just couldn't believe it.

'Iolanthe, the last few weeks with you in my life have been incredible,' Alekos said. His voice was husky, his eyes glowing like golden embers, everything about him intent and sincere. 'I want to spend the rest of my life with you and our son. Will you marry me?'

'I thought you'd already proposed,' Iolanthe half joked as she gazed in amazement at the gorgeous ring nestled in its black velvet box. A huge diamond was flanked by two winking emeralds.

'As you reminded me, that wasn't a proposal. It wasn't romantic.'

She jerked her gaze from the ring to his face. 'And now you want to be romantic?' She didn't know whether to hope or doubt.

'I want to give you the proposal you deserve,' Alekos answered smoothly, which Iolanthe, even in her stunned state of cautious happiness, realised wasn't quite the answer she'd have liked to have heard. 'So? Shall you try on the ring?'

Neither had he actually waited for her answer, she noted, and then told herself not to be so stupidly picky. Alekos was amazing. He was great with Niko. And most importantly, and alarmingly, of all, she loved him.

She loved him.

The realisation rocked through her. But was that reason to accept—or to refuse?

'Iolanthe?' The barest hint of impatience touched Alekos's voice. He took the ring from its box and held it out in silent command.

Wordlessly Iolanthe held her hand out and Alekos slipped on the ring. It felt heavy on her hand, the metal cold. She swallowed hard. She didn't know whether to rush in or pull back. She didn't know what Alekos felt.

Except she knew what he *didn't* feel.

'Perfect,' Alekos said in satisfaction, and Iolanthe smiled weakly. He raised his glass in a toast and she did likewise.

'To us,' Alekos said, and Iolanthe murmured her agreement. It appeared, she thought as she drank, that she'd just agreed to get married.

Her unease began to trickle away throughout the evening, due both to Alekos's thoughtful attention and her own inner pep talk. She could do this. They could do this. It was best for Niko, best for her. She could be happy with Alekos. She knew she could.

And when Alekos led her up to the hotel suite and took her in his arms, Iolanthe forgot all of her doubts. All of her fears. Here, in the shelter of his arms, accepting the promise of his kiss, nothing else seemed to matter.

She was still feeling the pleasant aftershocks of a night of lovemaking the next morning, as Alekos hit the shower and Iolanthe rolled over in bed, sleepy and sated and definitely happy. She lifted her hand to gaze at her engagement ring, a tremor of cautious happiness going through her at the sight. *This was really happening.*

A text pinged on her phone and she reached for it, wondering if it was Niko. She'd spoken to him last night before dinner, and he'd seemed happy to be at home with Amara. But the text wasn't from her son—it was from her housekeeper.

Please call. Niko frantic re PI.

Stunned disbelief and then dread crashed over her in an icy wave. Iolanthe sat up in bed. PI was Petra Innovation— but why would Niko be frantic? *What had happened?*

Her heart began to thud as she pressed the contact for home and waited for the phone to pick up five thousand miles away.

'Amara?' she said, her voice tight with anxiety, as soon as the housekeeper had said hello. 'What's going on?'

'Have you not seen the news?'

Iolanthe glanced at the huge flatscreen TV that had remained off the entire length of their stay. 'No...'

'Demetriou has done it,' Amara said grimly. 'He's shut down Petra Innovation.'

CHAPTER FIFTEEN

ALEKOS SMILED TO himself as he towelled his hair dry. He was humming, he realised. He was happy. Last night had gone perfectly, just according to plan. He and Iolanthe would marry.

This was how it was done, he reflected as he slung the towel around his shoulders and ran the water so he could shave. This was how to conduct an engagement, a relationship. Hassle-free, full of pleasure and enjoyment without any of the hang-ups or dangers of too much emotional involvement. Or love.

He cared about Iolanthe, yes, he could certainly admit that. And she cared about him. Maybe she even thought she loved him, but Alekos knew better. Love was weakness, exposure, pain. Neither of them had felt that last night. Neither of them would feel that ever.

Not if he had anything to do with it.

He was still humming when he exited the bathroom, his gaze searching out Iolanthe. He came to a stop, his insides icing over as he saw her, not lying deliciously rumpled and sleepy in bed as he'd expected and hoped, but standing by the bed, fully dressed, fists clenched.

'Iolanthe…?'

'Why did you do it?' Her voice came out in a furious whisper. 'How could you do it, Alekos? After everything? After…' She gestured to the bed, and then Alekos realised she was actually gesturing to the ring on her finger. And then she was pulling it off.

'What the hell…?'

'I have to say,' Iolanthe said, the ring now in one clenched fist, 'your timing sucks. You need to work on that. If you'd had any sense, you would have announced the closure *after* we'd said our vows. Made sure I really was trapped.'

'I have no idea what you're talking about,' Alekos informed her coldly. He could already feel himself going into shut-down mode in the face of her fury and contempt. It was familiar, this numbness; it was a comforting cloak instead of having your feelings flayed, your emotions stripped raw and your heart bared.

Iolanthe let out a hard, disbelieving bark of laughter. 'Can you really keep a straight face and say that? To *me*? We've been here before, Alekos. A night of passion that ends with you kicking me to the door.'

Fury beat in his blood. 'I'm not kicking you anywhere, Iolanthe. If anything, *you*—'

'You might as well be,' she cut across him, her voice savage. 'I'd rather you did! To act like everything is fine, when all along you'd been intending...' Her voice broke and he started to go to her, arms outstretched, everything in him wanting to comfort her.

She stepped away from him as if he'd become repulsive, her face twisting with contempt. Alekos dropped his arms, his stomach plummeting at the awful look on Iolanthe's face. She'd *never* looked at him like that, not even when he'd told her all those years ago that it was just sex between them, that they didn't have a relationship.

They had a relationship now, damn it, and it was tanking and he didn't know why.

'Iolanthe—'

'Don't touch me. Don't talk to me.' She held the ring out, her hand shaking, but Alekos didn't take it.

'I'm not taking that back,' he said as levelly as he could.

'It's over, Alekos—'

'It's not over until I understand what the hell is going on. We made love twenty minutes ago! And then I came out of the shower to this?' He flung a hand out, caught between fury and fear. 'What's going on?'

She stared at him, her face pale, her lips bloodless, her eyes like huge silver moons. 'Do you really not know?' she asked quietly. 'Are you really that…arrogant? Did you think it wouldn't matter?'

'Give me some clue as to what you're talking about,' Alekos said impatiently. But even as he said the words he had a plunging realisation that he knew exactly what she was talking about. The news had most likely come out this morning…and somehow Iolanthe had seen it.

'Petra Innovation,' she stated flatly, confirming his suspicions. 'That's what I'm talking about, Alekos. It was in the news this morning that you're still shutting down the entire company. In fact, you already have, and you let me find out—you let Niko find out—through the *news*.' She gazed at him, her eyes full of both hurt and hate. 'How *could* you? How could you do that to Niko, when you know how much he cares about the company?'

Alekos took a deep, steadying breath. He should have known Talos Petrakis would haunt him from the grave. The man had stolen everything from him, and continued to do so even in death. Except this, he acknowledged bleakly, was his fault. 'Iolanthe, I understand you're angry,' he said, keeping his tone careful and even, as if he were talking to a wild animal poised to strike or bite. 'But, please, let's talk about this reasonably.'

'Which just means you want to talk me round to your opinion,' Iolanthe surmised. 'Tell me this.' She levelled him with a look as honest and vulnerable as it had been ten years ago, when they'd spoken out on the balcony and he'd marvelled at how she could hide nothing. 'Did you ever intend *not* to close the company?'

Alekos stared into her mirror-like eyes that shimmered with angry tears and found he could not respond. He could not dissemble.

Iolanthe nodded slowly as a tear slipped down her cheek. 'I thought so,' she said quietly, and she held her hand straight out, releasing her clenched fist so the ring fell onto the bed. Then she turned to leave.

Alekos watched her go in appalled realisation. She wasn't just leaving the room or the hotel—*she was leaving him*. For good.

'Iolanthe, wait.' Startled out of his numbness, Alekos lunged for her. She shook his arm off with a snarl.

'Don't touch me.'

'What are you going to do?' Alekos demanded. 'Walk out into a strange city by yourself? How will you manage?'

'Better than you seem to think I ever could,' Iolanthe snapped. 'But then you've been managing me all along, haven't you?' And with an angry toss of her head she left, the slam of the suite's door ringing through the emptiness of the rooms.

Iolanthe stormed out of the hotel, hitting the muggy streets of New York with a determined, furious step that lasted twenty minutes before she slowed with a tired sigh. What was she doing? She needed to go back to the hotel, pack her things, find a flight, and get back to Niko.

When she'd spoken to Amara on the phone she'd said Niko had seen the news on the Internet and had gone into meltdown mode, a scenario which they'd avoided for months now. Iolanthe's stomach churned to think of her son dealing with this news alone, away from her for the first time ever.

And it was Alekos's fault.

She drew in a shuddering breath, the feelings of hurt and betrayal cascading over her again in a hot tide. How could he? And how could she have been so stupid to fall for him again, and far worse this time?

But she couldn't think about her broken heart or her shattered dreams right now. She needed to think about

Niko. Resolutely Iolanthe stiffened her shoulders and turned around to head back to the hotel—and Alekos.

She spoke to the concierge about arranging a flight back to Athens for that evening, her heart feeling heavier and heavier inside her. That done, she headed upstairs to face Alekos—and say goodbye.

She wasn't overreacting, was she? For a moment, as the lift soared skyward, Iolanthe let herself consider that question. Admittedly the whole situation had brought back raw feelings, painful memories. And maybe she should have kept from lighting into Alekos the moment he came out of the bathroom—but what really could he have explained? He'd shut down Petra Innovation, and, far worse, he'd done it without so much as a thought for her or Niko, for the family he'd been saying he wanted to have.

Some family. Sickly she remembered how Alekos hadn't even considered her point of view when she'd confronted him. He hadn't explained or apologised. And as the doors opened onto the top floor, she acknowledged that he'd *never* considered her point of view. He'd just persistently and determinedly waited for her to come round to his.

The suite was empty as Iolanthe walked through the rooms, her heavy heart now feeling as if it were coming up her throat. *Where was he?*

'Alekos…?' Her voice came out in little more than a whisper. No reply, and so she went to pack her things.

She came up short when she saw Alekos sitting on the edge of the bed, his shoulders bowed, his head in his hands.

'What…?'

He looked up blearily as she came into the room. His eyes were reddened, his expression haggard. He blinked a few times as if he couldn't believe she was there. 'I thought you'd left me.'

He sounded so despairing that she almost cracked. Almost rushed to him and put her arms around him, and pushed everything else aside. But, no. This wasn't just about her father's company; it was about them. It was, Iolanthe realised with total clarity, about what she wanted from a man. A marriage. And Alekos was not prepared to give it.

'I did leave you,' she said, her voice low. 'I came back to pack my things.'

He flinched as if she'd struck him, and again Iolanthe felt that surge of compassion, that need to comfort. She suppressed it and Alekos didn't say anything else. She moved past him, her hands trembling as she reached for a suitcase.

He was going to let her go. Stupidly, she wanted him to fight for her. For them. She wanted him to explain, to apologise, *anything*. It would take so little, but Alekos remained stubbornly silent.

But then, Iolanthe thought suddenly, if she wasn't willing to fight for them, why should she expect him to be?

At that moment she realised hollowly—she hadn't fought for anything before. A decade ago she'd let Alekos walk all over her, and then later her father and Lukas too. For ten *years*. And much more recently she'd still let Alekos call the shots even though she'd tried to assert herself in small ways. She'd thought the strong thing to do now was to walk away, but what if it was to stay and fight? Not just for her, for them, but for their family?

'Alekos.' She drew a deep breath and turned around. Alekos was still sitting on the edge of the bed, his head bowed. He looked defeated. 'Talk to me.'

He didn't even look at her as he answered. 'What is there to say?'

'Tell me why you have been so determined to destroy Petra Innovation.' As she said the words she realised there had to be more going on than she'd ever fathomed. She hadn't pressed Alekos on his history with her father, hadn't probed the nature of the vengeance he'd sought to wreak—all because she'd been scared to push him on anything. To upset the balance, to have him withdraw. 'Because you've never considered anything other than closing it down, have you?' she asked quietly. 'Not even for Niko.' It hurt to say it.

'Niko is my son,' Alekos returned fiercely. He raised his head, his eyes blazing. '*Mine.* Why on earth would I let Talos Petrakis take anything more from me?'

Iolanthe reeled back at the undisguised hatred in his tone. 'Alekos...what are you talking about?' He pressed his lips together, his expression closing down. Blanking her out, as he had before. But why? She felt a whole different kind of dread swirling in her stomach. 'I don't understand...'

'Maybe you don't want to,' he said shortly and rose from the bed, his back to her as he finished getting dressed.

The suitcase slipped from Iolanthe's fingers. 'What haven't you been telling me?'

'Nothing.' His voice was brusque, his back to her, and yet Iolanthe wasn't convinced. In that moment she realised how many things hadn't made sense. And she'd closed her eyes to it all—why? Because it had been easier. Because she was a coward.

But not any more.

'Tell me, Alekos. For my sake. For Niko's sake.' He said nothing. 'Niko is devastated,' she continued quietly. 'Do you realise that? He liked you. He *trusted* you. Do you know what a big deal that is to a little boy like him? And then he reads in the news that you, the person he's just let into his life, is taking the most important thing away from him—'

'It shouldn't be the most important thing!' Alekos interjected in a near-roar as he turned around to face her. 'It shouldn't be,' he continued in a quieter voice, but she saw the ravages of grief on his face and a cold feeling crept through her.

'Alekos, please. Tell me what is going on. What do you have against my family? My father?'

Alekos was quiet for a long moment as Iolanthe held her breath, waiting. 'I don't want to tell you,' he said at last. 'I don't want to hurt you.' He lifted a gaze so full of torment to her that Iolanthe's breath came out in a shocked hiss. 'And if you've already decided there is nothing between us...that it's over...'

'It's *not* over.' Alekos looked stunned and Iolanthe realised how fierce she had sounded. 'I don't want it to be. I...' Her breath hitched and for one second she considered all the times she hadn't said what was in her heart. 'I love you, Alekos. I want to fight for what we have. I know you don't love me back, but—'

'I do,' Alekos burst out. 'I realised that when you left. It felt as if the whole world had gone black. I love you, Iolanthe, and I can't bear the thought of you turning away from me again.' He let out a sound that was caught between a laugh and a sob, shaking his head as if he could deny the truth of what he'd just said. Wanting to hide his vulnerability.

'I won't leave you,' she promised. 'But you have to be honest with me, Alekos. You can't hold back. What is it you're keeping from me?'

Alekos sighed heavily and then sat next to her on the bed. He didn't speak and Iolanthe waited, both afraid and expectant.

'I worked for your father when I was twenty-two years old,' Alekos said. 'I had an internship, and he—he was like a mentor to me. I learned from him, and in return I gave him my ideas.' His mouth twisted with bitter memory. 'I presented him with an idea for a new software system.'

Iolanthe stared at him, transfixed. 'But what...what happened?'

'He listened to my idea. He made me go through the presentation twice and, naïve fool that I was, I gave him a DVD with the whole explanation on it. He promised me a full-time job with the company, assured me I was just the kind of man he was looking for.' Iolanthe heard bitterness in Alekos's voice, but, far more alarmingly, she heard pain. Raw, naked hurt, and it scared her.

'What happened then?' she whispered.

'He took my idea and had Callos copy it,' Alekos stated flatly. 'I didn't realise it at first, of course. He wrote me a letter—a form letter—terminating my internship and saying he'd presented my software system to his "team" and they didn't think it was workable. He was so sorry to let me down. Six months later Petra Innovation rolled out my system almost exactly, except not quite as good.' Alekos's mouth twisted. 'Callos tried his best, I suppose.'

'What are you saying…?' Iolanthe's mouth was so dry she could barely get the words out. 'My father *stole* from you? And Lukas helped him?'

He gazed at her bleakly, without hope or anger. 'That's exactly what I'm saying.'

Iolanthe sat there, her mind spinning with a thousand unwelcome new thoughts, unable to frame so much as a syllable. 'But why…? Why wouldn't he just let you work for him?'

'He was threatened by me,' Alekos said with a shrug. 'It was the only thing I could think of. He wanted someone he could control. Someone like Callos.'

'But—'

'You don't believe me,' Alekos cut her off, his voice flat.

'It's not that simple,' Iolanthe protested numbly. 'I don't know what to believe. I'm in shock, Alekos. Give me a moment, please.' She struggled to make sense of it all, battling an instinctive refusal to believe what Alekos was saying…and yet she did believe him, because she knew he wouldn't look like this, so utterly without hope, if what he was saying wasn't true. But what that meant about her father, her whole life...

She closed her eyes, too stunned to deal with the emotions coursing through her. 'Why didn't you tell me before?' she finally asked.

'At first because I didn't think you'd believe me. And then later because I didn't want to hurt you.'

'And you didn't think shutting down my father's company would hurt me?' She shook her head. 'Hurt Niko?'

'Not in the same way,' Alekos defended himself. 'Niko will have a much bigger, better company, Iolanthe. His true birthright. Why can't you understand and accept that? I'm not denying him anything—'

'You think bigger is better?' Iolanthe closed her eyes, suddenly too tired to argue any more. 'Alekos, it's not even about the company. The truth is I was facing the prospect of selling it anyway, because Lukas ran into so much personal debt.'

Alekos's eyes widened. 'What? Why didn't you tell me?'

'You're not the only one who can hide things, I suppose,' Iolanthe answered. 'I didn't tell you because I didn't want to feel more beholden to you. Weaker.'

'But if you were thinking of selling the company anyway, why are you so angry?'

Alekos sounded so bewildered Iolanthe almost laughed. Or cried. Because even now he didn't get it. 'Because it's not about the company anymore,' she said wearily. 'Or at least not just about that. It's about us—about trust and openness and love. What kind of relationship can we have if you won't let me in? If you won't trust me with the truth? If you won't enter into a conversation with me about something so important because your mind is made up and bent on revenge?' Her voice rose. 'Because this is about revenge, isn't it, even though my father is dead and the only people you're hurting are the ones you claim to love? You still need your vengeance.' She shook her head, filled with weary despair. 'Where is love in that scenario, Alekos? Where is there room for it—for me, for Niko? Did you even think what this would do to him? Hearing it on the news, knowing that you hadn't bothered to explain *anything* to him?'

Alekos's face contorted. 'I didn't think about that,' he admitted. 'I didn't let myself think of it. I convinced myself that this was separate from us—from all of us.'

'Because you've tried to make it separate. You've put your need for revenge into a box and refused to let anyone have so much as a look-in.'

'This wasn't about revenge so much as justice,' Alekos said in a low voice that throbbed with feeling. 'I've waited a long time for it, Iolanthe—'

'But he's *dead*,' she burst out, tears trickling down her face as fresh pain mingled with old grief. 'He can't touch you now, and you can't hurt him—'

'Do you *know* what your father did?' Alekos cut across her, his voice savage, his face twisted in awful memory. 'All of it? He tried to ruin my company. He discredited me to everyone that he could. He did his absolute best to keep me from succeeding in *anything.*' Bitterness scored every word that spewed from his mouth. 'After he saw me with you, he had me beaten. *Beaten*, like I was a dog, in a back alley, even though by that time I had my own company, I was a man in my own right—'

The blood drained from Iolanthe's head as she stared at him in horror and still the words kept coming. 'I wanted to work for him because I thought he could be a father figure to me. I thought he was a hero. *My* hero. I built him up in my mind and he played right into my stupid fantasies, calling me the son he'd wished he'd had. And then he stabbed me in the back. In the heart. I tried to get a job at another firm and they turned me away because your father had whispered in their ear. Everyone's ears, it seemed. He did his damned best to destroy me, which made him worse than my own father, who was only indifferent—' He broke off gasping, throwing a hand up to his face.

'I didn't know...' In that moment Iolanthe realised how much it had cost Alekos to admit this. Proud, strong Alekos, felled by weakness, hurt by love. 'Oh, Alekos.' She went to him, her heart breaking just as his was from all these revelations. 'Oh, Alekos. I'm sorry. I'm sorry I didn't know...'

'It's not your fault,' he muttered, tensing away from her, but Iolanthe put her arms around him anyway.

'No, but I'm sorry for the pain my father caused. I'm sorry for the pain *I* caused, making it worse by not knowing. I wish you'd told me.' She pressed her cheek against his back, her eyes closed. 'I wish you'd told me.' Yet would she have believed him? Would she have accepted it? She could accept it now, years after her father's death, the pain and grief old and starting to heal. But maybe she wouldn't have been able to back then. Who could say?

Alekos was silent, his body shuddering with the aftermath of revealing so much, and Iolanthe wondered where they went from here. *How* they went. What did they build their future on *now*?

'We need to fly back to Athens,' Alekos said eventually. 'I'll talk to Niko.'

Iolanthe's arms tightened around him. 'What will you tell him?'

Alekos turned to look at her, the ravages of emotion still evident on his face. 'The truth,' he said. 'Don't you think it's time we all knew the truth?'

A little over twelve hours later Alekos was walking into Iolanthe's town house, her hand held tightly in his. He was clutching her hand hard, he realised, craving her support. Her love.

The journey from New York to Athens had been tense,

with Iolanthe worried about Niko and Alekos having no idea what the future held for any of them. Would his son reject him now? Would Iolanthe?

He felt as if he were seeing the world with fresh eyes, eyes that weren't filmed over with bitterness and hate. Iolanthe had been right; he'd let revenge guide him for so long. It had twisted his logic, his whole mind, into a bent shape that he hoped Iolanthe's love could straighten out. If she was patient enough with him. But after everything that had gone before he wondered whether he deserved it.

The town house was quiet as they entered, and then Amara appeared from the kitchen, scorching Alekos with a single burning look before she addressed Iolanthe.

'He's upstairs. He hasn't spoken or eaten all day.'

Alekos's insides clenched hard at those words. *This was his fault.*

'Come on,' Iolanthe said softly, and, still holding his hand, she led him upstairs.

Niko wasn't at his desk as he'd been the last time Alekos had been up there. No, now his son was lying on his bed, his skinny knees tucked up to his chest, his narrow back to them.

'Niko,' Iolanthe said softly, and Alekos heard the clogged sound of tears in her voice. 'Niko, we're home.'

Niko didn't answer; he didn't even move. Alekos stepped forward. 'Niko, it's me. Alekos. I...I wanted to talk to you about what you heard about Petra Innovation.' Niko's shoulders tensed, rising to his ears, but he still didn't say anything. 'I'm sorry, Niko,' Alekos said, and now his voice was sounding clogged. 'I'm sorry for not thinking through what I was doing. I'm sorry for hurting you. So sorry.' His voice broke as he realised afresh how his actions had affected his son—and Iolanthe. The two people he loved most in the world. He'd let his need for revenge cloud everything, distorting his view of the world. Of what was important. 'Hurting you is the last thing I'd ever want to do,' he said in a low voice. Niko didn't answer, and Alekos dropped to his knees by the bed, resting one hand lightly on his son's bony shoulder.

'Niko, I think I know a little bit about what you're feeling,' he said, and from behind him he heard Iolanthe draw a short, surprised breath. 'I think I know because I felt it a bit as a child. Like…like I didn't belong.' Even though Niko hadn't moved or spoken Alekos could tell he had his attention now. 'I felt like I didn't belong because I was different from everybody else,' he continued. 'I lived with a family that wasn't my own, and it was hard. Sometimes it felt easier to bury myself in books—books about computers—than try and make people accept me.' He felt his chest go tight. 'Make them love me.'

Niko rolled over so he could look at Alekos. The uncertainty Alekos saw in his son's face made his chest go even tighter. 'Did they love you?' he asked quietly.

'Not the way I wanted. I had to wait a long time to find a family to love me, Niko. A long time. But I think I've finally found one.' Niko's eyes narrowed and Alekos continued, 'You. You and your mother are my family now.'

Niko's expression remained narrowed as his gaze searched Alekos's face for understanding. 'We are?' he finally asked, his voice full of equal measures of hope and doubt.

'You are.' Alekos squeezed his shoulder lightly. 'If you'll have me.' There would be time later to explain to Niko that he was his true father. Time to explain how and why everything had happened, and to strengthen the bonds Alekos knew were already there between them. Strained, fragile, but there.

'Why did you shut Petra Innovation down?' Niko asked in a small voice.

'Because I wasn't thinking.' Strange how his determination to have his revenge seemed so petty and pointless now. 'Because I thought other things were more important than family and love.' He smiled at Niko. 'Now I know differently.'

'Will you keep it open?' Niko asked. 'Will you stop it from closing?'

'If that's what is best for everyone,' Alekos answered. 'I want to do what's best for you and your mother and for us as a family.'

Niko frowned uncertainly. 'But we aren't really a family...'

'We will be,' Alekos promised, his voice choking. 'We will be.'

EPILOGUE

One year later

THE WAVES SHOOSHED gently onto the sand as Iolanthe came out onto the terrace, the cool evening breeze caressing her face. Alekos turned to her with a smile as he held out a drink—lime juice and tonic water, in consideration of her current state.

'Is Niko asleep?'

'Yes.' Iolanthe rested a hand on her burgeoning belly as contentment stole through her veins like warm honey. She had so much to be thankful for.

The last year had been one of both challenges and joy. She and Alekos had married, a quiet ceremony with only Niko and a handful of friends in attendance. Alekos had kept Petra Innovation open, turning it into a branch of Demetriou Tech that focused on mobile apps. Several of Niko's were marketed through it and made a tidy sum that Alekos put into a trust for his son.

Niko had started to blossom under the care and love of both of his parents, and a new doctor had helped him make stronger attachments and cope with life's challenges. He'd started a new school and was beginning to adjust. It hadn't always been easy, and Niko sometimes took as many steps backwards as he did forwards, but...they were getting there. And the journey was more than worth it.

Now they'd taken a few weeks out of their busy lives in Athens to spend some family time on Alekos's island. And their family was expanding...not just with the baby she carried, but with Alekos's siblings. He'd made some initial inquiries to find his sister and brothers, and if all went well he'd be meeting them again soon. Yes, there was so much to be thankful for.

'I love this place,' Iolanthe said as she joined Alekos at the railing. 'It's so peaceful.'

'Being here always reminds me of when I first fell in love with you,' Alekos answered with a smile. 'Although maybe that happened on a different terrace, outside a ball-room in Athens.'

Iolanthe laughed softly. 'That might be a bit of revi-sionist history, Alekos. I think you fell in lust with me there, not love.'

'I'm not sure about that.' Alekos rested his hand on top of Iolanthe's, lacing his fingers through hers as their baby, due in three months, kicked beneath their joined palms. 'I think I was just in denial.'

'Maybe I was too,' Iolanthe murmured. 'But not any more. Now I'm just happy—and thankful. So, so thankful.'

'You and me both,' Alekos answered, and, touching her chin, he tilted her face up for a kiss that lingered as the moonlight spread its first silver rays over the placid sea, and serenity settled on the world.

* * * * *

*If you enjoyed this story, check out these
other great reads from Kate Hewitt*
MORETTI'S MARRIAGE COMMAND
INHERITED BY FERRANTI
LARENZO'S CHRISTMAS BABY
Available now!

And don't miss these other
SECRET HEIRS OF BILLIONAIRES
themed stories
THE SECRET TO MARRYING MARCHESI
by Amanda Cinelli
BRUNETTI'S SECRET SON
by Maya Blake
Available now!

MILLS & BOON®
Hardback – September 2016

ROMANCE

To Blackmail a Di Sione	Rachael Thomas
A Ring for Vincenzo's Heir	Jennie Lucas
Demetriou Demands His Child	Kate Hewitt
Trapped by Vialli's Vows	Chantelle Shaw
The Sheikh's Baby Scandal	Carol Marinelli
Defying the Billionaire's Command	Michelle Conder
The Secret Beneath the Veil	Dani Collins
The Mistress That Tamed De Santis	Natalie Anderson
Stepping into the Prince's World	Marion Lennox
Unveiling the Bridesmaid	Jessica Gilmore
The CEO's Surprise Family	Teresa Carpenter
The Billionaire from Her Past	Leah Ashton
A Daddy for Her Daughter	Tina Beckett
Reunited with His Runaway Bride	Robin Gianna
Rescued by Dr Rafe	Annie Claydon
Saved by the Single Dad	Annie Claydon
Sizzling Nights with Dr Off-Limits	Janice Lynn
Seven Nights with Her Ex	Louisa Heaton
The Boss's Baby Arrangement	Catherine Mann
Billionaire Boss, M.D.	Olivia Gates

MILLS & BOON®
Large Print – September 2016

ROMANCE

Morelli's Mistress	Anne Mather
A Tycoon to Be Reckoned With	Julia James
Billionaire Without a Past	Carol Marinelli
The Shock Cassano Baby	Andie Brock
The Most Scandalous Ravensdale	Melanie Milburne
The Sheikh's Last Mistress	Rachael Thomas
Claiming the Royal Innocent	Jennifer Hayward
The Billionaire Who Saw Her Beauty	Rebecca Winters
In the Boss's Castle	Jessica Gilmore
One Week with the French Tycoon	Christy McKellen
Rafael's Contract Bride	Nina Milne

HISTORICAL

In Bed with the Duke	Annie Burrows
More Than a Lover	Ann Lethbridge
Playing the Duke's Mistress	Eliza Redgold
The Blacksmith's Wife	Elisabeth Hobbes
That Despicable Rogue	Virginia Heath

MEDICAL

The Socialite's Secret	Carol Marinelli
London's Most Eligible Doctor	Annie O'Neil
Saving Maddie's Baby	Marion Lennox
A Sheikh to Capture Her Heart	Meredith Webber
Breaking All Their Rules	Sue MacKay
One Life-Changing Night	Louisa Heaton

MILLS & BOON®
Hardback – October 2016

ROMANCE

The Return of the Di Sione Wife	Caitlin Crews
Baby of His Revenge	Jennie Lucas
The Spaniard's Pregnant Bride	Maisey Yates
A Cinderella for the Greek	Julia James
Married for the Tycoon's Empire	Abby Green
Indebted to Moreno	Kate Walker
A Deal with Alejandro	Maya Blake
Surrendering to the Italian's Command	Kim Lawrence
Surrendering to the Italian's Command	Kim Lawrence
A Mistletoe Kiss with the Boss	Susan Meier
A Countess for Christmas	Christy McKellen
Her Festive Baby Bombshell	Jennifer Faye
The Unexpected Holiday Gift	Sophie Pembroke
Waking Up to Dr Gorgeous	Emily Forbes
Swept Away by the Seductive Stranger	Amy Andrews
One Kiss in Tokyo...	Scarlet Wilson
The Courage to Love Her Army Doc	Karin Baine
Reawakened by the Surgeon's Touch	Jennifer Taylor
Second Chance with Lord Branscombe	Joanna Neil
The Pregnancy Proposition	Andrea Laurence
His Illegitimate Heir	Sarah M. Anderson